Love . . . a long time coming.

The sight of Paul sitting up, alive, gave me a rush of gratitude so intense I reached out and put my hand to his face. "Don't ever scare me like that again," I said in a wobbly voice.

He put his hand over mine, cupped my fingers with his fingers, and leaned into my palm. His cheek was warm. I listened to the wood crack in the fire, felt the connection of our hands and the wind ruffling my hair. Something was taking shape inside of me, a kind of courage, a willingness to be foolish, and it was slowly forming out of the knowledge that I had been lonely for a long time.

"I don't want to lose you," I said.

Lois Gilbert

River of Summer

AN ONYX BOOK

ONYX
Published by New American Library, a division of
Penguin Putnam Inc., 375 Hudson Street,
New York, New York 10014, U.S.A.
Penguin Books Ltd, 27 Wrights Lane,
London W8 5TZ, England
Penguin Books Australia Ltd,
Ringwood, Victoria, Australia
Penguin Books Canada Ltd, 10 Alcorn Avenue,
Toronto, Ontario, Canada M4V 3B2
Penguin Books (N.Z.) Ltd, 182–190 Wairau Road,
Auckland 10, New Zealand

Penguin Books Ltd, Registered Offices:
Harmondsworth, Middlesex, England

First published by Onyx, an imprint of New American Library,
a division of Penguin Putnam Inc.

First Printing, August 1999
10 9 8 7 6 5 4 3 2 1

Printed in the United States of America

PUBLISHER'S NOTE
This is a work of fiction. Names, characters, places, and incidents either are the product of the author's imagination or are used fictitiously, and any resemblance to actual persons, living or dead, events, or locales is entirely coincidental.

ACKNOWLEDGMENTS

For their sensitive, insightful, and thoughtful response to this work I give thanks to Wayne Oakes, K. C. Grams, Miriam Sagan, Lesley King, John Thorndike, Claire Kelly Gilbert, Mary Gilbert, Chris Bauerle, Liz Reidel, Shel Neymark, Walter Cooper, Doug Bland, and Billy Halsted. For their faith and vision I thank my agent, Ken Atchity, and my editor, Audrey LaFehr. For teaching me how to canoe and survive the storms on the river, I thank Beverly Antaeus.

Prologue

At first I couldn't believe it was my father's voice on the telephone. It had always been my mother's job to call us, a detail in her housekeeping to be performed once every two weeks, usually on Saturday morning. But this was Tuesday afternoon. I sat on the floor of my empty house and thought, my mother is dead.

"Is Mom all right?" I asked him, once we'd greeted each other.

"She's fine." Richard's voice was soft, the enunciation careful. The hard drinking hadn't started yet; it was early in Connecticut. "Have I caught you at a bad time?" he asked.

I smiled. My marriage, career, and emotional state had all been shattered in the last six weeks, but I realized this was a more specific question, a point of etiquette rather than a real inquiry.

"Of course not, Dad. How are you?"

"Fine, just fine. Your mother told me about your plans."

There was a longish pause as I tried to decipher where he was going with the conversation. It didn't take him long to come out with it.

"Are you sure it's too late for you and Jake?"

I looked around at the bare walls, the stripped floors. "He's gone, Dad. I don't want him back."

"I'm sure you could convince him to return, Zoe. Beg him. Appeal to his sense of duty. Get on your knees if you have to."

"He's having a baby with another woman," I said. Could my mother have failed to mention this? "That's not something I'm going to overlook."

"Jake's place is with you."

"Not any more, Dad. I'm sorry."

"So unfortunate," he said. "I don't know how you'll manage."

"I've managed without him for a long time. He was rarely here."

"And you're going through with this plan to run away from all your responsibilities in Santa Fe?"

"If I want to come back I will. I still own the company."

"I worry about you, traveling by yourself."

I'll bet you do, I thought. It was something

my mother would never be able to contemplate. I'd always wondered how much of her illness was the result of his desire to have her stay put.

"How's Mom?" I asked.

"Amelia's fine," he said, sounding irritated. "You're the one I'm concerned about."

"Is she still in therapy?"

"As long as there's money to be milked from our savings, your mother will find the charlatan to take it. I can't understand that woman's eagerness to impoverish us."

"You can afford it."

"This last one is an idiot," he grumbled. "According to your mother he wants to schedule a session with me. Can you imagine?"

"No," I said. It was true, I couldn't.

"Come here for a visit," he said. Not a request. A summons. In thirty seconds he'd made me feel like a failure, a ghost of the awkward child I'd been. My chest tightened, and even though I was determined to carry out my plans, I knew my voice sounded high and nervous. "I can't right now. I'm headed west, to the Grand Canyon, Canyonlands, San Francisco. I'll stay with Marta for a few days."

"Are you sure your sister has the time to be with you? Your mother says she's very busy."

"Maybe later in the summer I could come

out." It was a safe lie, one I'd been telling for years.

"I suppose it's useless to talk to you, then," he sighed.

"I'm glad you tried, though," I said. I took a deep breath. "I love you, Dad."

"Stay in touch," he said, and hung up.

One

Route 160 was empty. It was hot. I flipped on the air-conditioning, set the cruise control at sixty, leaned back, and watched the wind comb the clouds into long strands. In this corner of Arizona I was in another country, the sovereign state of the Navajo reservation, but it could have been the moon, with oxygen. The earth looked naked, with long stretches of mesa that curved into buttes and arroyos the color of flesh.

After twenty minutes, the Percodan unleashed a steady warmth that crept through my bloodstream, and my jaw relaxed. The Winnebago was like a metal womb, enclosing and protecting me, and my breathing was deeper now. In the late afternoon light every rock and telephone pole and clump of snakeweed was haloed, and I felt muffled from thoughts that could cut me. Out here I could believe I was Zoe Harper, not that married lady with the hyphenated last name, but my old maiden self, hyphen gone, husband gone, the core of me still here even if it was under heavy medication.

A silhouette appeared in the hot rippled air at the horizon, a young man with his thumb out, standing next to a Ford Pinto with the hood propped up. His hair was lit by a radiant Percodan-assisted brightness, giving him a halo that looked almost supernatural, but that didn't stop me. I passed him without touching the brake and an instant later the Winnebago was airborne.

"Jesus!" I braced myself against the steering wheel as the RV slammed back to the pavement, then skidded to a halt a few yards past the Ford.

In the side view mirror I could see the young man running toward me. He was shirtless in the heat, with a red duffel bag hitched across his shoulder. A long blonde braid flopped up and down on his back as he ran. The halo worked at a distance, but as he came nearer I could see his face was smeared with grease. Without pausing for permission he opened the door and swung into the passenger seat.

"Thanks," he said, stashing his duffel behind the seat. "You saved my life."

"What did I hit? Are you all right?"

"Yeah, I'm okay. You just ran over my bag, that's all."

"What the hell was your bag doing in the middle of the road?"

He gave me an idiot's grin. "Guess I must have left it there."

"You scared me to death."

The grin faded into an anxious look. "If you could take me to Moab I'd be really grateful."

"No," I said.

"Why not? I'll pay you for gas."

"I don't pick up hitchhikers."

"I don't bite. I could even help you drive."

"You can call for a tow," I said, pointing to my cell phone.

He shook his head. "She's a wreck now. Transmission's busted."

"You're just going to leave it here?"

"The tribal police will put the word out, get it hauled away. Somebody will take the tires. They have a few miles left on 'em."

"If you don't want to use the phone, get out. Please." My heart started knocking wildly in my chest.

He looked out the window and took a deep breath and let it go. "It's hot out there."

"If you want me to call somebody, I will."

"I need a ride, not a tow truck. Couldn't you make an exception, just this one time?"

"Sorry."

His hand curled around the door handle. He looked at me. I could feel him looking. I turned my face away and stared through the windshield and tried to look as though I were breathing normally. A long moment passed and then the latch clicked open. When he slammed the door shut I glanced up to see the back of his hand pressed against the window, middle finger raised.

My cheeks burned. I revved the motor, put the Winnebago in gear, and pressed the accelerator to the floor. In the side mirror I could see him running after me, yelling. I didn't look back again. No more stopping for strangers. Not on this road.

Before Jake moved out I'd rarely taken an aspirin, but that changed. Right away I started to have little accidents: I cut my finger, burned my arm, twisted my ankle. For the first time in my life I bought first-aid cream, iodine, Band-Aids, extra-strength Tylenol, and Ace bandages. I avoided hurting myself the way other people quit smoking: It took serious effort. It required thought, internal threats. For weeks I was on the tightwire of functioning adequately until I wrecked my car on April Fool's Day. That was almost a month ago. Since then I'd been taking six tablets of Percodan a day for whiplash. Sometimes seven or eight, if I couldn't stop thinking about Jake.

At least I owned a house on wheels, six thousand pounds and twenty-one feet of recreational vehicle. Although it was depreciating by the minute, it was all mine, a home I could take with me, and I kept telling myself it was the only home I needed. I was perfectly happy to putter along in a small, functional Winnebago, with no history attached to it at all.

An hour later the Utah state line went whizzing by and a roadside park appeared on the right. I slowed, then pulled into a space near the restrooms. My neck ached, and ached, and ached, broadcasting pain like a child who can't shut up. There was only one pill left. One pill, I thought: I'll never make it. I shook it into my mouth and crunched it between my teeth. The bitterness soothed me, and I slid my tongue over my gums to find every particle, then ran a finger along the inside of the bottle and licked the dust from my knuckles.

Whenever the pills faded from my body, I cried a lot. Any old thing could set me off. Yesterday it was the thought of the glass jars of preserves I used to keep on a shelf above the stove. I remembered how the morning sun came flooding through the windows and those jars glowed like jewels. I loved canning. The harvest from the garden always thrilled me—the extravagance of it, the gift of so much from such little seeds. When the snow was thick on the flowerbeds, I could open a jar of my apricot marmalade and Jake and I could have it on toast every day for a week, a piece of summer in the middle of January. Even now I could stop and take a jar of it out of the tiny cupboard above my tiny sink, that very same jam, warm and golden and true, but my hunger was gone. And it was the hunger I missed.

Ever since I was three years old I'd cut out pictures of warm crowded rooms in houses, bedrooms with bright braided rugs, forsythia outside the window, an overweight cat sitting like a sphinx on a bureau. I wanted to make homes, and I did, not just for myself but for other people. I'd bought and sold thirteen houses in Santa Fe over the past twenty years, most of them melting adobe ruins in the barrio along Alameda, south of the river. The first house I bought hadn't been lived in for eleven years, and when I flushed the toilet the bowl broke in two pieces. I installed a new toilet, replaced twenty-seven broken window panes, knocked down the ceilings, and replastered each room by myself. When the house finally sold, I made enough to hire most of the labor on the next one and let my fingernails grow.

Jake was amazed, at first, that I knew how to lay pipe and tile and wire. In time the novelty of a wife who could use a blowtorch wore off and I think, ultimately, it disturbed him somewhere deep down in his testicles. Jake wrote computer programs at Los Alamos, and his hands were always softer than mine. I ran a crew of eight men who could tear out the guts of a house and rebuild it from the inside out, and Jake used to make fun of them in a way that was too aggressive to be casual. I knew it bothered him that I depended on them, not him. I was just not helpless enough for him. This is what I told myself in the lazy riffs of Percodan thinking, and it helped.

When we first met, Jake told me I had the face of a state fair queen, but in the last year a sprinkling of gray hairs had appeared in the crown of my head, too many to pluck, white as salt. Under my sunglasses, bruises from the accident still darkened the skin around my eyes, and whenever I glanced in a mirror I felt sorry for the stranger I saw. Then I'd remember who it was.

My fortieth birthday loomed on the horizon, only six months away, and I looked forward to it about as much as a case of typhoid. But being thirty-nine was worse. It was a joke, a ridiculous age, claimed year after year by Jack Benny until he died of being thirty-nine. Thirty-nine tipped me forward into the Sahara of the forties, a drying up of all the juices. No one was called "promising" after they hit that mark. No one had "potential." When a woman hit forty, she became invisible.

Three o'clock: By three-thirty I'd be ready to drive again. I crawled into the back to lie down and stepped on a red duffel bag that hadn't been there before.

The bag.

The bag belonged to the boy who had given me the finger.

What I had done dawned on me slowly, and my face grew hot as I stared at it. I wondered if he'd notified the police. I didn't want his bag. It was a mistake. I lifted it, hoping it was light and filled with nothing more than dirty laundry, but it was heavy. Maybe it was full of drugs: bags of cocaine, bricks of hashish. Maybe I should throw it away.

I tugged the zipper.

A billfold lay on top of his clothes, containing a checkbook with no name or address printed on the checks. A California driver's license lay behind a clear plastic protector. The boy's name was Paul Griffin and his address was a rural route in Petaluma. The slots next to the license held a Visa card in his name, a senior lifesaver's certificate from the Red Cross, and an expired student ID from the University of California at Berkeley. Two hundred and eighty-five dollars lay behind the leather flap.

I pulled out a fleece vest that was neatly folded on top of the clothes. I liked the color, a deep teal green. A few pairs of his jeans lay underneath and I looked in the waistband of one of them to see what size he wore. Before long I was sitting in front of a pile of six T-shirts, a sleeping bag, one shaving kit, a pair of binoculars, green windbreaker, three pairs of shorts, a tangle of socks, and some underwear that had seen better days.

There was a knapsack on the bottom, and when I unzipped it and looked inside I saw a brown paper bag that had been rolled open and shut so many times it was soft and wrinkled as cloth. It contained something firm, like small paperback books, or decks of cards. When I peeked inside I saw money: stacks of bills, each stack wrapped in a rubber band. I shook the money out of the bag and riffled through it, checking denominations. Mostly hundreds and fifties and twenties. He had about a hundred thousand dollars here. My hands started to sweat.

I put the billfold and the clothes back in the order I'd found them and patted everything flat on top so it would look untouched. Let him be there, I thought, let him be waiting by his wreck of a car so I can get rid of all this and drive away.

The cholla made long shadows as I gunned the motor over a rise and sped back toward Arizona. If Paul Griffin was gone, could I trust the tribal police with a hundred thousand dollars in their lost and found? I could mail the bag to the address on his driver's license, but what if he didn't get mail there anymore? What if there was no forwarding address?

After an hour of driving I saw the car a quarter mile ahead, the hood still raised, but no sign of the boy. I pulled over across from the car, stepped out on the pavement, and crossed the highway. Broken glass glittered on the shoulder and the tar was soft with heat. When I peered in the open window I could see him curled up on the back seat, sleeping. I knocked on the roof.

"Excuse me," I said. He stirred and his eyes opened. They were a clear, perfect blue, the skin around them unlined.

"I have your bag."

He blinked, then nodded.

"I'll go get it."

I turned around and walked back across the road to the RV. I heard his car door open and when I looked back he was hitching up his jeans and shaking out his legs. He was barefoot.

"Watch the glass," I said.

He stepped delicately around the shards and crossed over to the RV. "I still need a ride."

"I don't pick up strangers."

"Paul Griffin," he said, extending a hand.

"I'll get your bag," I said, ignoring his hand. I unlocked the side door of the Winnebago and stepped into the main cabin.

"Let me help you," he said, coming in behind me.

I edged past him and backed out the door. He emerged with his duffle and smiled. "Thanks."

"Will you be all right?" I asked, feeling foolish.

"I don't know."

"What will you do?"

He flashed me a smile and revealed a set of milk-white teeth. "Whatever I want."

A truck appeared at the crest of the hill, a gasoline tanker. Paul crossed the road and stood next to his car, barefoot, duffel in hand, thumb out. The truck gathered speed on the downhill slope and passed between us without slowing. The wind of its passing shook the earth and sand swirled across the road in its wake. Paul put his bag down and wiped grit from his eye.

"Maybe I'll wait until somebody stops for you," I called to him.

He looked up and down the empty highway. "Suit yourself."

We stood there, facing each other, twenty feet of bleached asphalt between us. He didn't resist my being there, and he didn't invite it. He seemed to have given up on me. I was adrift in the Percodan high by now. Nothing mattered too much, but it was hard to leave.

I licked my lips. "Are you thirsty?"

He reached into his car and held up a plastic water bottle. "Want some?"

"No," I said. "I have water."

A raven tipped its wings above us and flew behind a rise. A minute went by. "I could eat," he said.

"Would you like some raisins?"

"Okay."

I fished a box of raisins out of my purse and walked over to his side of the road.

"We have to stop meeting like this," he said.

"I looked in your bag," I said.

He narrowed his eyes and shook a few raisins from the box into his mouth. "I'm not surprised."

"Where did the money come from?"

He wiggled his eyebrows, which were darker than his braid.

"Tell me," I said.

"I'll tell you if you take me to Moab."

"No."

He tapped a few more raisins out of the box and handed it back. "You ever hitchhike?"

"Sure," I said. "Constantly."

"That trucker would have stopped for you. Girl like you, dressed nice, good legs—"

I kept my expression bland and suspicious, but I loved being called a girl.

"—you could be a psychopath with an Uzi up your skirt, but you'd get a ride. Guy like me on a road like this, they could find my bones here, you know? Because nobody's gonna trust me."

"Ah."

"So you have a real opportunity here. You could do a good deed. I'd even pay you for it."

"How much?" I was curious.

He shot me a look. "Fifty bucks."

"How far is Moab?"

"Hundred miles? Hundred and fifty?"

"You'd have to put on a shirt," I said.

Paul unzipped his bag, pulled out a T-shirt, shook it out and slipped it over his head.

"And shoes."

He rolled his eyes but opened the car door, sat on the seat and pulled on socks and sneakers. There was a subtle lift in my spirits, as if I had just paid for a ticket on a roller coaster. Now I had to take the ride.

It was strange to have company in the cab of the Winnebago, and in spite of the Percodan my body was alert to his every move. From the corner of my eye I could see the hairs on his forearm, the place on his wrist where his diver's watch had slipped down, exposing white skin. He smelled like sun screen.

"About the money," I prompted him.

"What's your name?" he asked.

I watched him warily from the corner of my eye as he twisted around in his seat. "Zoe Harper. Just tell me you got it legally. Tell me I'm not abetting a felon."

"So where are you from?"

"Santa Fe. Did someone give it to you? Or did you earn it?"

"I won the lottery."

"Right."

"About four years ago. They send me seven grand every month."

"You make seven thousand dollars a month and you drive a Pinto?" I didn't believe him for a second.

"I buy a junker when I need one, run it ragged for a couple of months, maybe a year, until it breaks down. Then I get another one."

"Doesn't it worry you, not knowing when your car's going to die?"

"It's a way to meet people," he said. "What are you doing out here all by yourself?"

I laughed, but the question annoyed me. I'd have to think of interesting lies to tell people when they asked.

"You look married," Paul said.

"I was," I said.

"You split?"

"I was replaced."

"Oh."

It had been almost two months since Jake told me his mistress was pregnant. One minute I was scraping his leftover eggs into the sink, the next he was telling me he had a lover and she was pregnant. But I'm your lover, I almost said. When he told me he wanted to marry her and have the baby, I couldn't seem to get any air in my lungs and had to walk around the kitchen twice to encourage the air back into my chest. "You must have known," Jake had said. "You weren't blind."

Now I slanted a look at Paul, who was wrapped in silence, staring out the window. Lottery, my ass. He was probably a thief.

I counted ravens. Nine ravens later, Paul lifted the lid of my cooler and held up a banana. "Want one?"

I shook my head.

"Can I?" he asked.

I nodded.

"I got married once," he said.

I smiled. "You look like you're about twenty-two years old."

"Hell no, I'm twenty-eight. My girlfriend and I got drunk one night in Reno and went to one of those quickie wedding chapels. Bang, we were married. We were underage, just seventeen."

"What happened?"

"Her dad got it annulled. She cried at the time but married the golf pro at her country club about six months later. I think she's about to have her second kid."

"Glad to see you escaped without too many hard feelings." I gave him a look over the tops of my sunglasses.

"I'm mature for my age," he said breezily, tearing open a bag of pretzels.

"I'll take some of those."

Paul passed the bag over to me. We were quiet for a minute or two, watching the bare rock mesa rolling by.

"Did you get a good settlement from your ex?" Paul prodded. "Make a lot of money in the divorce?"

Alarm rippled through me, an instinctive certainty that wariness was called for. The way he asked that—wasn't the tone a little too casual? The countryside was desolate, mile after mile of gray blackbrush, no gas stations and no cars. It could be days before anyone saw my dead body.

"What?" I asked.

"You must be rich, traveling alone like this." He threw his arm over the back of his seat and looked back at the carpeted indulgence of the Winnebago.

"I'm not rich," I said. My neck was rigid. Maybe that's where his money came from, I thought: dead women. I could stop and jump out and run. There was money hidden in the glove compartment. He could have that.

"Do you see a gas station up there?" I asked.

"You need gas?"

"I need to use the bathroom."

"Then pull over." His voice was flat.

I kept the needle on sixty.

"Am I making you nervous?" he asked.

"I'm fine."

"You seem nervous."

The severe shape of the land offered no shelter, no trees. "How far is it to the next town?" I asked.

"Why do you want to know?"

"Just tell me!" I snapped.

He took out the map in the slot by my chair and unfolded it. "We're somewhere between Cow Springs and Kayenta. It's a ways, maybe thirty, forty miles. We're in the middle of the Navajo reservation."

"I know that."

"Are you upset about something?"

I tightened my lips and stared at the double yellow line.

"Well, let me know when you get over it," Paul said mildly, untying his sneakers. He propped his feet on the dash. His socks were white with blue stripes around the tops. I glanced at his feet in their white socks and relaxed slightly. I could smell them. They smelled clean and human.

"Sorry," I said, and twisted my neck to the right and the left, stretching out the tension.

"You have any kids?" he asked.

"No. Jake hated kids."

"So why'd you split up?"

"He knocked up his mistress."

"And she's having it?"

"Oh yeah," I whispered. I could feel tears needle my sinuses and made my voice hard. "He's going to be a terrible father. He can't stand to hear a baby cry."

"Then he's in trouble."

"He's the kind of man who has to have his sheets ironed. I had to physically stop him from straightening pictures in other people's homes. Can you picture somebody like that having a baby at fifty-five?"

"I don't know. People change."

"Oh, he'll change," I said grimly. "He'll be the father of the year. He'll have a goddamn breakthrough, just to spite me."

I was aware of Paul watching me, trying to figure me out. It was strenuous trying to talk to him. I didn't want him to know me. For a week now I'd had the Winnebago to myself, and to have Paul in it felt like being caught in an elevator with someone I wasn't sure I liked.

"So you hate men now?"

"No," I lied. "They're okay."

"You buy into that Mars and Venus stuff? Think we're from different planets?"

"I don't think it matters," I said. "I think we're stuck with each other."

At dusk we saw the swirling blue lights of state troopers on the highway ahead of us. A car had collided with a truck hauling an open wooden trailer full of sheep. The trailer had tipped over and twenty or thirty sheep were bawling and staggering toward the ditches on both sides of us. Paramedics loaded a stretcher into the back of an ambulance. I came to a halt next to one of the officers and rolled my window down.

"You'll have to go back, ma'am," he said. "Unless you want to wait a couple hours."

"Do you need any help?" Paul asked.

The trooper smiled. "No thanks, son. We got it covered."

"Is there a way around?" I asked.

"There's a county road about a mile south. Follow it west, across the arroyo and up a bluff until you see another road heading north. It'll get you back to the highway eventually."

It took a minute or two to jockey the Winnebago back and forth to turn us around. Stars were beginning to prick the navy sky. Moab was only twenty miles away, and it seemed unlikely that the detour would take long. In another hour we'd be in town and I could dump Paul at the bus station or rental car place or wherever he wanted to go.

The detour led us down a washboard dirt road that rattled the dishes in the cupboard. I crossed the arroyo, climbed to the top of the bluff and lurched along for half an hour without seeing any road signs. We came to an unmarked fork.

"Which way?" I asked Paul.

"Right?"

I turned right and we crawled over ruts for another thirty minutes, up and down piñon-studded hillsides. "Maybe we should have turned left," I said.

"I don't see any of these roads on the map."

"Should I go back?"

"Yeah, go back."

"It'll be a bitch to turn this thing around," I said.

"Okay, keep going."

"The road has to go somewhere, right?"

"We could stop for the night. Camp out," he said.

"Here?"

"Why not?"

"Not here."

"Okay."

My headlights made a slender cone of illumination in the darkness. The trees were black, and it was hard to gauge the depth of the ruts. Thirty minutes later there was still no sign of the highway, and I felt a sharp impatience with the whole day. I'd been driving since dawn and now I was lost and Paul Griffin was still in my Winnebago and I wasn't ever going to get rid of him.

The bottom of the RV scraped the high island between two ruts and I had an image of the oil pan torn open, bleeding vital fluids. When I pressed the accelerator there was no forward motion, just a whir of wheels digging a hole in the sand.

"I'm stopping here," I said.

"In the middle of the road?" Paul asked.

"We're stuck." I unbuckled my seat belt and stepped out.

Paul remained inside. "Just give it some gas."

I shook my head. "That's going to make it sink deeper. I'll jack it up tomorrow morning, cut some branches and get them under the wheels, but I don't want to go tripping around these rocks in the dark."

We were parked under a cottonwood that must have been over a hundred years old. It was at least five feet across at the base. When the wind rustled its leaves the tree sounded like water rushing over rocks, the click of its branches like pebbles knocking in a stream. The sky was thick with stars and a lone jet blinked along the Milky Way. Venus was bright as a candle. The night was cool, and I reached behind the seat for my jacket as Paul came around the nose of the Winnebago.

"I'm starved," he said.

"There's a can of stew in the cupboard above the sink. You might find some crackers and cheese in the refrigerator."

"You want me to make you something?"

"Okay."

I leaned back against the flank of the Winnebago, road weary and tired of talking to Paul, tired of being cooped up in the front seat with him. I was not in the mood to be kind.

"This cheese smells bad," he called from the cabin.

"Throw it out," I said.

He came out the side door and pulled his arm

back, elbow cocked, danced forward a few steps and hurled the brick of cheese past the apron of light. There was no sound of it hitting the ground.

"I didn't mean that literally," I said.

Paul shrugged. "Birds will eat it." He walked back inside, brushing crumbs from his hands.

When I came in he was holding the empty vial of Percodan in one hand, squinting to read the label. Damn, I thought. I'd left the bottle in the silverware drawer, not expecting a nosy hitch-hiker to be rooting through my kitchen. He tilted his head and looked at me.

"Why are you taking this stuff?"

I grabbed the container from him and rummaged in the debris between the front seats for my purse. "That's none of your business."

"How much do you have left?"

"None," I said. "I had the last one this afternoon." What was he thinking, that I'd give him some?

"You been taking it long?"

"No. A couple months."

He winced. "Didn't anyone tell you it might be a rough ride coming off these?"

"How would you know?"

"I spent some time in rehab."

"When?"

"Just once. Junior high. My best friend started dealing coke and I got caught up in it. It only took my dad about a week to figure out what I was doing, and then he put me in a clinic. There was a woman in there, trying to get off Demerol. I think her name was Mary, but it could have been a fake name. Anyway, she was a doctor, and she knew a lot about commercial drugs. She said prescription painkillers were worse than heroin. Pain candy, she called it. She couldn't leave it alone."

"I'm not a junkie, Paul."

He held up his hands, palms out. "I believe you. But I know what I know. You got any vitamin C?"

"I think so."

"Start taking it. A thousand milligrams every four or five hours."

"Is that supposed to cut the craving?" I was being sarcastic, but he didn't take it that way.

"Not really. But it can't hurt. You're going to want to take something, and if you swallow vitamins on the same kind of schedule you took this stuff, at least your mouth can pretend you're still supplied."

"Don't worry about me," I said. "I'll be fine."

"That's what all the junkies say. You sure this is the last of it?"

I folded my arms across my chest and stared him down.

"Okay, okay. You'll be fine."

We ate in silence, and I was relieved that Paul didn't try to clutter dinner with small talk. I poked at the canned stew, ate white things that could have been onion or potato while Paul chewed and swallowed and stared out the black window. When we were finished I washed the plates, dried them, put them back in the cupboard. He wiped the counters and put away the bread and butter.

"I want you to sleep outside," I said.

He looked at me in amusement, as if I had a more carnal imagination than he did. I turned away and brushed my hair energetically while he dragged his sleeping bag from the duffel and headed out the door. When the door closed behind him I ransacked the drawers until I found a bottle of Vitamin C, unscrewed the cap and shook two tablets into my palm. I chewed them. There was a tart pain as they stung in my mouth, more bitter than the pills I missed, but familiar all the same.

Even when Paul was gone I could feel the

glow from his duffel bag and all those neatly stacked bills in the brown sack. The lottery. I didn't believe him, but I didn't think he was the type to knock over a bank either. Where did the money come from? Maybe it wasn't even his, maybe he was taking it somewhere for somebody else. That thought chilled me. I didn't want to be in the loop of anyone's money laundering.

I shut the door on my speculations about Paul and resolutely turned my mind to Marta, my little sister. She was expecting me in San Francisco next week. The last time I'd seen her she'd been on a stage outside the Palace of Fine Arts, dressed only in strategic loops of electrical tape, a black cobweb connecting her to eight other naked women. They'd chanted "Stop" over and over again in amplified whispers that sent prickles up the back of my legs. The troupe had been mentioned in *Art Forum,* and it looked like Marta had arrived at a certain level of celebrity in performance art circles.

My sister was bisexual and glamorous in a pierced eyebrow, black lipstick sort of way. She had tiny breasts that I envied. No sag, no fat anywhere on her. I had a more fulsome figure and tried to hide it in solid, dependable looking suits when I wasn't wearing overalls and a painter's cap. I liked to be covered up. Even when she was fully dressed, Marta looked as if her clothes might fall off any minute. I loved her more than anyone on earth, and I was headed to San Francisco to cry on her shoulder and spend a few days bashing Jake.

The space between the bed and the ceiling of the RV was claustrophobic and I was so wide awake it was hard to shut my eyes. At three a.m. I took another two tablets of Vitamin C. Sleep didn't come until just before dawn, and even then I was jumpy, my mind like a fish on a line, jerking from one dream to the next, tethered to a craving I couldn't appease.

Two

In the full light of morning I felt washed out and pale, and when I looked at myself in the mirror on the closet door I did not look good. My hair had flattened down on one side and licked up on the other, giving my whole head a lopsided slant. Without makeup my features disappeared and my face seemed naked, but it seemed absurd to go into the bathroom and apply mascara before I went out to jack the RV out of the sand. There was a rip at the neckline of my robe that I'd ignored for months, but now I fingered it self-consciously. I changed quickly into jeans and a T-shirt and sneakers.

Percodan would have smoothed over everything—the way I looked, the awkwardness of a stranger beyond the door, waiting for me to come out. My whole body yearned for pills. Just thinking about them, I could almost smell the faint bitter scent of the opened bottle and imagine the taste, the promise of drowsy indifference. My mouth watered, thinking about it. I grabbed the bottle of vitamin C, shook a little pile of tablets into my hand and put all but two in the pocket of my jeans. It made me feel better to have them close, crunching against each other on my hip. I swallowed the two that were left in my hand.

When I emerged into the cool of the morning with my toolbox, I saw the Winnebago was nestled like a whale in a dip at the bottom of a slope. Paul was awake, stretched out full length under the cottonwood, hands loosely clasped behind his head, but still in his sleeping bag. His long blonde hair was tangled, his blue eyes vacant as the sky.

"Morning," I said. "Can you give me a hand?"

He scrambled out of the bag and I was relieved to see he was wearing sweat pants. "Sure. What's up?"

I put the toolbox down, opened it, and took out a hatchet. "I need some branches to put under the front wheels. Pine is better than cottonwood. Go cut about fifteen branches, no more than an inch thick, as long as your arm. I'll jack it up while you're cutting."

Paul held the hatchet as if he'd never seen one, as if it were a toy. "Cool." He grinned at me.

"You want some gloves so you don't get pitch on your hands?"

"Okay."

I handed him a pair of leather gloves and took some out for myself. "Scoot," I said, when he didn't move. He waved the hatchet and walked off while I lifted the jack and slung it across my shoulder.

The Winnebago had sunk to its front hubcaps in the sand. I scraped away loose dirt to level the base for the jack, then placed it under the bumper and cranked the RV up until the front wheels were in the air. I was ready for the branches, but Paul was nowhere in sight.

I found him fifty yards away in an arroyo, using the hatchet as if it were a saw. He was gnawing away at a piñon branch that had bent almost in two without breaking.

I smothered a smile. "The wood's too green to break. Bends like rubber. Would you mind if I try something?"

Paul wiped his arm across his forehead. "Go ahead."

I raised the hatchet and chipped the branch off in two strokes. "It needs a little momentum.

Put some muscle into it." I handed the hatchet back to him.

He saluted me with the blade, then turned to the tree. "Here?" he asked, grabbing the base of another branch.

"That's good," I said. "You don't have to hold it. Just strike close to the trunk."

His strokes were tentative at first, but within a few minutes we had a pile of clippings.

"That's enough," I said, and gathered them in my arms. Paul tossed the hatchet up in the air and caught it by the handle. I took it from him and shook my head. "You're going to hurt yourself."

"Not me," he said, prancing down the slope ahead of me. "Just call me Paul Bunyan. You can be Babe."

"Who's Babe?"

"My big blue ox."

"Gee, thanks," I said.

We packed the boughs under the wheels and I lowered the RV until the branches cracked from the weight and the jack slid out.

"You're a handy woman to know," Paul said. "Who taught you to do this stuff?"

"Me." I was out of breath, and I wanted to finish the job. "I don't like to depend on other people." I walked around and opened the door on the driver's side. "Hop in. We need your weight."

I fired up the engine and felt the tires spit out a few branches before they gained a purchase on the debris we'd packed under them, and then the RV swayed and grumbled its way out of the hole. I drove a few feet out on the hardpan before I shut off the ignition.

"Voilà," I said. "Ready to go."

"Can we have some breakfast first?"

"Sure," I said. "Just don't take too long. I'm eager to get back on the road."

We sat down across from each other at the table. Paul ate cereal and read the back of the box. I unfolded the map and snapped off the cap on a container of yogurt.

"The first thing we need to do is find out where we are and then leave," I said.

"We must be in Canyonlands."

"How do you know?"

"Look at the map. We left 191 and headed west for at least an hour. That would put us inside the park," he said.

I was impressed that he knew we'd been going west. In the dark, west felt the same to me as east, and even during the day I had a hopeless sense of direction unless the sun was rising or setting. Some people seem to have a compass in their bones, a physical recognition of true north planted in the column of their bodies. I wasn't one of them.

"If we went back the way we came we could get back to the highway. The sheep must be gone by now," I said.

"That road sucks. Besides, didn't you come this way to see Canyonlands? It's here. We're here. Why not look around?"

"We're in the middle of nowhere."

"Come on. I want to show you something. You'll be surprised."

He stood and walked out the door, and I reluctantly slid out of my seat to follow him.

"Just follow me to the top of this rise," he said.

We walked thirty yards uphill and came to a spot that overlooked the plains to the north. The view was immense, a wide ocean of land that rolled in waves to the horizon. In the middle distance the spires of the Needles district thrust upward like the arms of a congregation lifting its arms in prayer. The sky was a blue vault of infinite proportions, vast, clean, and blue, unmarred by a single cloud. At the far edge of the plains I could see lavender silhouettes of mountains that were at least a hundred miles away.

Maybe a hundred and fifty. I took a deeper breath and some tension unlocked itself in my chest.

An assortment of bike trails threaded the bare hills below us. The road ahead switchbacked two or three miles down to the highway. In the valley a city glittered in the yellow morning light.

"Moab?" I asked.

"Moab."

The road showed little sign of regular use. No tire tracks but ours were visible over ruts that meant erosion rather than traffic. Clumps of grass and cottonwood seedlings were scattered up and down the slope. It was a lovely day.

We went back inside and sat at the table. Paul ate his cereal. I felt an odd sense of disappointment because we weren't lost, there was no danger, and it was time to drive into the city.

"I bet if we hiked for half an hour we could see the Colorado River," he said.

A flash of interest overrode the subtle sense of being manipulated.

"Why would we do that?"

"Don't you have any curiosity at all?"

"So we'll go there, then leave."

The spoon was halfway to his mouth, dripping milk. "Okay."

I took a red felt-tip pen from my purse and traced the route to Moab, made an X, then continued the line to San Francisco.

We'd been walking for an hour and eighteen minutes across the slickrock desert, the back of our legs colored by red dust as Paul led us toward the burnt cliffs to the west. I walked gingerly around rocks, afraid of hurting myself. Sword-bladed yucca and scattered clumps of blackbrush offered no shade, no coolness to the eye. At least a dozen trails crisscrossed ours, none of them with any visible destination.

"Are you sure this is the way?" I asked again. In my new trekking shorts and sneakers and T-shirt with the Grand Canyon logo I felt ridiculous. I had a blister on the inside of my baby toe. The last time I'd walked this far—well, I'd never walked this far. I'd never liked walking on dirt. I worked in the dirt, I built homes on dirt, but dirt had always meant the job was unfinished, the house unlandscaped.

"You're doing great," Paul said.

I limped behind him, balking. "How much farther?"

"Be careful," he said, sliding down a scree-covered slope.

I skidded on pebbles the size of ball-bearings

and felt my feet fly out from under me. My tailbone smacked the hardpan and my hands hit the ground and burned.

"Paul!" I snapped.

"Yeah?" He was forty feet ahead, turning to look at me but still moving.

I picked myself up. It looked flatter down where he was, the pale line of the trail level on the slickrock. "Wait!"

"Are you okay?" he asked, slowing to hear my reply.

"Where is this river, exactly?"

He stopped and hitched up his shorts and scratched under the waistband. Then he waved at the entire western horizon. "Somewhere that way," he said.

"You don't know?"

"Are you thirsty? Want a drink?" He slipped the daypack off his shoulders, unzipped it, and pulled out a water bottle.

I felt like hitting him. "Please tell me you know where we're going."

Paul unscrewed the cap of the water bottle. "Give me your hands," he said. I turned my hands up and saw that both palms were scraped with pinpricks of blood dotting the skin. Paul poured a thread of water into each palm.

"We'll turn back if you want," he said. "But I think it's right over there."

I blew across my hands and assessed the distance. "I want to go back."

"Okay."

"You can go on if you want."

"Okay." Paul took the water bottle, screwed the cap back on, put it in his day pack, shouldered the pack, and kept on walking.

He pissed me off, and that gave me energy.

An hour later we were both sitting on a ledge, a thousand feet above the confluence of two rivers.

Every cell in my body was screaming for Percodan by now. "You dragged me all the way out here for this?"

Paul sighed. His hair was sweaty around his baseball cap. "Shut up, Zoe."

"You shut up."

He was silent, which enraged me.

"If you'd told me how long this would take I would never have come. I'd be halfway to California by now." I was shocked at the things I couldn't stop myself from saying. It's his fault, I told myself.

"I didn't know how far it would be. Besides, you didn't have to come. You could have turned back."

"And wait all day for you to show up?"

"Whatever." The weariness in his voice made me want to pull his hair. I folded my arms across my chest and watched a raft full of brightly colored passengers bobbing down the river a thousand feet below. The sun was directly overhead.

"Can we go now?" I asked in a tone I regretted as soon as I heard it.

Paul opened his pack and pulled out two sandwiches wrapped in plastic. "I made this for you," he said, handing me one.

I took it, aggravated by his thoughtfulness. Peanut butter and jelly. I unwrapped it and bit it. The landscape looked old and bald and burnt in layers of rust and faded green, the horizon stretching away to Nevada. Something hard inside me unclenched a little as I let my eyes wander over the bleached rock walls below us. A flock of birds flew up the river, white as paint against the dark water. I looked at Paul, who had already devoured his sandwich and was lying in the searing afternoon sun with his shirt open, his hairless chest smooth and tight with muscle. His belly was flat, with a trickle of blonde hair pointing downward. I turned my face back to the rivers coming together below us.

Paul propped himself up on one elbow, opened the water bottle, and passed it to me. "Have a drink."

"Do you want the last bite of this?" I held out a piece of sandwich. He nodded, opened his mouth. I put it in. He chewed it. I took the water bottle, held it to my lips, and drank.

When I came out of the shower I went to the closet to grab my jeans and get some more tablets of vitamin C. Paul was outside, talking to three kids on mountain bikes. They were his age, three young men balanced on bicycles with nubbly tires, holding their balance with tiny movements forward, then back, as if they had too much energy to stop and put their feet down. They had calf muscles the size of cantaloupes.

I stepped back against the wall to avoid being seen, popped two tablets in my mouth, and chewed them. Paul was laughing at something one of them had said, and his gestures were like theirs—loose and uncensored and graceful. He lifted a shoulder and scratched his armpit. As I watched him I touched my throat and felt a wistfulness that surprised me.

One of the bikers lifted his chin toward the Winnebago and asked a question I couldn't hear. "Yeah," Paul said, "We bought it just last week. Rides real good. Heavy on gas, though." He kicked the dirt, hands in his pockets. I smiled in the shadow of the door. When the bikers left, Paul strode back to the RV, a swagger in his walk.

He was startled to see me standing there, and the tan on his face turned a shade darker as he blushed. "Have a nice chat?" I asked.

He shrugged, opened the refrigerator, and hid his head in it. "We need more food," he said. "Good food. No more of this cardboard prefabricated canned trash you call dinner. I want some basil, figs, prosciutto, real butter. You don't even have any good bread."

"For what?"

"If we stay another night."

"I thought you wanted to go to Moab."

"Just for supplies. This place is perfect for at least a couple more days. Let me cook for you."

"You cooked last night," I pointed out.

"That's not cooking. That was survival."

"You think you can find prosciutto in Moab?"

"I know just the place," Paul said.

Exercise is a funny thing, how it can make the endorphins sing in the blood. I felt almost good, but I knew in a few hours I'd start thinking about Percodan again, and I didn't want to be alone and think about it. I wanted to hike again. I wanted to feel the sun burn my skin and I wanted to walk so hard I couldn't remember what I was walking away from.

"One more day. Then we leave."

The main street in Moab was lined with billboards that catered to mountain bikers, rafters, canoeists, and hikers. With Arches and Canyonlands so close, and two of the largest rivers in the West meeting just south of town, it was a tourist mecca. The Colorado River provided a higher water table for the area than we had in the high desert of Santa Fe. The trees were taller than I'd expected, and I could smell the river in the dry air, a fragrance of mud and willow.

Paul guided me to a grocery-delicatessen a few blocks past the visitor center. The facade was so nondescript I would have missed it without his directions, but when I opened the screen door I could see the tiny store was packed with people.

Cheese and sausage dangled in net bags from hooks in the ceiling, and a clerk slung articles over to the cashier without much regard for the heads of the customers, who had to duck. Three glass showcases featured different cuts of meat, fish, and salads. Paul took a basket from the stack by the door, wove his way through the throng, and waited his turn in the line. When he finally caught the attention of one of the girls behind the counter, he ushered me in close so I could see, his hand warm on my back. When he pointed to an item he checked my face, and I nodded at each selection. The girl behind the counter wrapped what he'd chosen: two loaves of bread, olives, prosciutto, marinated artichokes, smoked turkey, linguine, and three kinds of cheese.

"We'll never be able to eat this much," I said.

"I bet you five dollars we will." He picked up the pile of packages she'd heaped on the counter and turned to let the next customer take our slot.

"Do you drink wine?" he asked.

I shrugged. "I don't need any."

He picked a bottle from the shelves, and I read the label over his shoulder: Villa Antinori Chianti Classico.

"Maybe we should get two," he said. "This isn't a bad price." The bins of produce along one wall caught his eye, and he placed carrots, onions, garlic, and a small head of butter lettuce in the basket.

"Smell this," he said, picking up a bouquet of basil from a basket by the cash register. There were small white blossoms just coming out on the tip of each stalk. I buried my nose in the fragrant leaves and kept my face hidden for a moment while the sharp, familiar ache began to swell in my chest, as if a chunk of glass had lodged itself just above my heart. In my old kitchen I'd kept a pot of basil in the window. It was my favorite herb, and I hadn't smelled it or tasted it since I'd put the house on the market and emptied all the rooms.

It wasn't until Paul had criticized my canned dinners that I realized I'd been living like a refugee. I'd lost more than a husband; my old pleasure in food, in cooking, in the simple sensual art of living, was gone. I'd lost the feeling that I deserved to eat a good meal. I'd probably lost fifteen pounds since Jake left.

"She likes it," he said to the clerk. "Give us two bunches."

The bill came to over a hundred dollars, and I let him pay it.

By the time we got back with groceries the light had ripened to a rich golden color, giving the agave and rabbitbrush a seamless, butter-yellow halo. The wind had died to a rare stillness. There were thunderheads on the horizon, but the sky above was open and empty while the mountains were translucent, turning violet in the distance.

"Terrible things can be beautiful in the right light, if you get far enough away," I said. I stared out the window at the purple horizon while Paul chopped an onion.

"Like what?" He mashed a few cloves of garlic, tossed the skins away and melted a cube of butter in a pan. Once the butter was bubbling he added the onion and garlic, then sat down to mince the basil. I watched him work, a kitchen towel slung over his shoulder, and thought, this is nice.

"What things look beautiful if you get far enough away?" he insisted. "Tell me."

"Strip mines. Highway cuts. Tent caterpillar infestations." I sat across from him at the dinette, my face resting on my knuckles.

"Is that what you're doing?" he asked. "Getting far away?"

"You eat a lot."

"Aren't you hungry?"

"Rarely."

He leaned back in his chair and grabbed a loaf of bread from the counter. I watched as he cut two pieces, then slathered both with the butter he'd set out on a plate to soften.

"Sourdough," he said. "Try it." He held one

slice by the corner and flopped it on the table in front of me. I gave him a look but held my tongue and pulled myself up to get a plate and a knife.

"How far do you think we walked today?" I placed the bread on the plate and cut it into four squares.

"Seven or eight miles."

I looked out the window while we chewed together in silence. The sky had deepened to rose. Nighthawks were diving in the falling light, skimming for gnats.

"Where's your corkscrew?" he asked.

"I think there's one in the drawer by the sink."

Paul opened the bottle of wine and took a deep sniff, then poured us each a glass.

I licked my fingers. "I think that trick with the vitamin C helped."

"Good. I felt like I was hiking with a junkie coming off a four-day binge."

I swirled the wine in my glass. "Who taught you how to cook?"

"That's a long story."

"I've got time."

"The first time I ran away from home—"

"The first time? You did this often?"

"Don't interrupt. Yeah, I did, every chance I

got. The first time I ran away from home I hitchhiked from San Francisco to Brooklyn. I'd heard there was a shipping office there that hired for Danish, Swedish, and Norwegian ships in the merchant marines. The Norwegians hired me on as galley boy for a freighter that crossed the Atlantic twice a month. They eat well, and the chef was brilliant. He's cooking for the French embassy in Washington now."

"How old were you?"

"Fourteen. There's no age limit for most European lines, no need to be in the union. Most of their captains start out that young." He turned back to the stove and shook the handle of the pan to flirt up the onions.

"So you dropped out of high school?"

He shrugged. "I only lasted a year at sea before my dad tracked me down and hauled my ass back to California. I made up for the school I'd missed in one summer."

"Your parents must have been frantic."

"I'll never regret going. The middle of the ocean is still my favorite place in the world. But the work is endless. When I wasn't peeling potatoes I was chipping rust and painting. Maintenance is hell on a tub made of steel that sits in salt water all the time."

"Why did you run away from home?"

Paul added the basil to the pan and scooped the butter over the minced leaves. "My father is not a nice guy."

"How so?" I took a sip of the wine. It was rich, fruity, a soft explosion of flavor on my tongue. I waited for Paul to reply. It took a while.

"He hurts people."

"How?"

"By abusing his power, that's how. He's a subtle bastard. Out to control whoever he can."

"Hard to imagine anyone controlling you," I said.

Paul snorted. "He tried hard enough. But my mom was the real casualty. She used to be a nightclub singer. Hot stuff in the Bay area, a headliner in the old days, even had a chance to tour in Vegas. My dad squashed that idea. He couldn't stand to have other men look at her, and after he married her, he made sure she quit."

"He must have loved her."

"That's not love. He was jealous of her. He didn't want her to go anywhere without him. She was completely dependent on him. She never even drove a car."

"She doesn't sing anymore?"

"She doesn't do anything anymore. She's dead." His voice was cool, indifferent.

"Oh." I wished I hadn't asked. "When did she die?"

"A long time ago. When she quit singing she got throat cancer."

"I'm sorry."

He kept his face turned away from mine as he measured ingredients into a bowl. "Now he wants me to be the same buttoned-down pillar of the community he thought my mom should be. But it killed her. I know it did. I'm not going to get in the cage he built for her. It would kill me too."

What he said made me uneasy. It sounded like the kind of excuse any dropout would use. "What do you think your mother would have wanted for you?"

Paul shook his head. "Doesn't matter now, does it? She's gone." He sounded angry.

There was a pause, and I didn't want to be the one to fill it. So you have wounds too, I thought, and there was a certain satisfaction in seeing them, however bitter.

"This knife is not sharp," he said, as if it were a crime.

"There's a sharpener in the drawer."

There was a clatter of silver as he rummaged

in the drawer until he found what he was looking for, and then he drew the knife across the steel rod in the rapid, staccato motions of an expert.

As Paul sliced the ham into translucent strips I considered my own father and how I'd run away from him. For the past twenty years Richard and I had been polite, at best. But even when he was polite I could feel the iron of his will opposing mine, wanting to keep me as small as my mother. When I was around my father I felt myself shrink into the wall, reduced, poised to disappear. Until he'd called me last week, this was the sum of our interactions: He gave me hundred dollar bills and I took them.

But after I'd put the whole country between us and thought I was free of him forever, I'd found a man who was just like him, a domineering, unfaithful liar. I wondered if my father had ever knocked up any of his mistresses. For all I knew I could have a dozen half brothers or sisters.

"Your appetizer is ready, ma'am." Paul set a plate between us on the table with six dark, plump bundles arranged on it. He handed me a fork.

"What is it?" I asked.

"Figs stuffed with pesto, wrapped in prosciutto. Try it."

I cut one with my fork, speared the morsel, and brought it to my mouth. It was exquisite. A flicker of greed aroused my taste buds and I wanted more. It was an odd feeling, unfamiliar, and it took me a moment to identify it. For the first time in months, I was hungry.

The next day we hiked through a canyon of mushroomlike formations that loomed above us, massive as trees made of stone. The rocks were twisted into unlikely shapes from time and wind, bright red at the base and capped with white limestone. Our destination was the top of a ridge spiked with pillars, and when we reached it we were rewarded with a sweeping view to the south and east. Snow-capped mountains glimmered at the horizon, beyond the maze of canyons below us.

At the top of the ridge the wind was gusty, scouring my legs with grit, but in the eastern sky a flare of light had fractured into a small, oval rainbow against a film of cloud.

"See that?" I asked Paul.

"What is it?"

"A sun dog. I've never seen one that low on the horizon without it bringing a big wind."

"Bigger than this?"

"Much. Maybe some rain, too. Those clouds are thickening in the east."

"You're a weather fanatic?"

"I've had to be. In the building trade I had a lot to lose from a cloudburst if the roof wasn't done or the stucco hadn't set. Besides, I like weather. It's always moving."

"I guess we should head back."

"It won't hit for at least an hour."

"You can tell all that from a spot of color in the sky?"

I smiled. "Wait and see."

As we walked back, I could feel the sunburn on my shoulders. My sneakers were rusty with dirt and my eyes were locked in a squint against the light and wind.

It had never occurred to me before to walk for the sake of walking. If I were at X and wanted to go to Y, why not drive? If I were going to X only to return immediately to Y, why bother? I was used to working all day on my feet at a job site, filling in for anybody who had to leave or never showed up, running back and forth to Furrow's for nails or tools or stucco or lumber. I was too tired at the end of one of those days to take a walk.

The landscape was beautiful but monotonous,

the rise and fall of the slickrock unrelieved by much vegetation or wildlife. I walked and thought about what we'd eat for lunch and whether or not I'd put sunscreen on the back of my neck. I thought about the slump in Santa Fe real estate and whether or not it would last long enough to let me back into the game. The day I bought the Winnebago I'd called each member of my crew and told them I was leaving for good. They told me I'd be back, I could change my mind if I wanted to. It was the wanting to that was missing.

Walking felt feminine, close to the ground, slow and watchful. When I was little my father taught me how to steer a canoe down the Housatonic River as if there were no more essential art in the world than the J-stroke. We took a week-long trip for my eleventh birthday and paddled a hundred miles down the Allagash River in Maine and camped out every night. There was a snapshot from that trip I kept in my address book; it showed the two of us paddling away from whoever took the picture. It was my favorite photograph of my father, even though it didn't show his face. He was like God to me in those days, before he started drinking, before my ideas of how I wanted to live my life changed from his.

Walking reminded me of canoeing. My arms used to stroke a blade through water as regularly and rhythmically as my legs now scissored over land. I would like to canoe again, I thought. It was a skill I hadn't used in thirty years.

Of course I thought about Paul as we walked, but I didn't want to. Out here his stacks of money seemed like colored paper, unreal and unthreatening. I didn't want to carry them around in my head or wonder where they came from. Most of the time we were silent. At first the silence between us felt empty, like a bare cupboard, but after a while it lost that enclosed and vacant feeling and spread into the rocks and sky and stumps of trees, and silence became the thing I needed most.

After we'd been walking for an hour the storm slipped out from behind the ridge. The sky grew dark and violent, the wind shrieked across the bare rock and whipped our clothes. It began to rain. It was one thing to watch weather through a window, but walking in it was a shock. In two minutes I was wet, cold, and scared.

"I hope this doesn't last," I said.

Paul must have heard the fear in my voice. "It's okay. We'll get a little wet and a little cold, but we'll be all right."

He wasn't careful. He didn't see how a bad

thing might happen. We were going down a steep hill when he called back to me, "Run! Just let go. Let gravity help you."

"No way," I said.

"Your feet know how to do it."

"I'll meet you down there."

"It's when you try to stop that you fall."

I ran just a little, until I got scared, and he laughed and plunged on ahead, heels flying.

In the morning the sight of him was like a cool, wet rag placed on my forehead, medicating me with his youth and his lack of ambition.

"One more day?" He was smiling, sure of himself now.

"One."

We had to drive into Moab to fill the water tank and recharge the batteries, and I let Paul take the wheel for the first time. He was excited. I felt perfectly relaxed. After putting the RV into reverse to back out of our space, he braked more sharply than I expected, and then I sat up in the passenger seat, erect and anxious.

"Slow down!" I barked at him as we rattled down the dirt road. My voice was shrill, edged in panic.

Paul muttered something under his breath, his elbow slung out the window, eyes hidden behind his sunglasses. He sank back in the driver's seat and twisted his baseball cap until the bill hung down his neck.

"There's a stop sign ahead. Slow down, Paul." I fought to lower my voice, keep it neutral.

"You mean that stop sign down there that's a quarter mile away?" His foot tapped the accelerator and the Winnebago lurched forward.

"Yes, damn it. Now quit playing games. Slow down."

He gunned the motor and sprayed gravel, twisted the wheel back and forth until the RV was swaying from side to side, skidding slightly on the outside curves. The dishes crashed against each other in the sink. He almost hit the stop sign, then laughingly brought the RV to a halt in the middle of the intersection.

I unbuckled my seat belt and leapt out, slamming the door. I stalked over to his side, flung open his door, and stood glaring at him.

"Out," I said.

"Come on. It was a joke. I'll be good."

"No. No. No. Is that clear enough for you? You blew it. You are never driving this thing again."

"Fine. I'll walk." He swung out of the driver's seat and struck off down the dirt road, away from me.

"Asshole," I called after his retreating back.

* * *

When I got back from Moab, he was gone. His duffel was still behind his seat in the Winnebago, so I assumed he'd return after he'd punished me long enough. The sun was going down. I felt a queasy uncertainty about whether or not I'd been right. How fast had he been going, really? Thirty? Thirty-five? But it was a lousy dirt road, with potholes and loose gravel.

The greens and mustards of the desert faded until dusk swallowed all color and left only gray. It was black outside when Paul reappeared, and even though my face must have glowed with relief, he didn't speak to me, he just took his sleeping bag and went out the door.

In the morning I cut a peach into six sections, arranged the pieces on a small plate and offered it to him when he came in for breakfast.

"You can be a real bitch," he said.

"I know," I said. "I've had lots of practice."

Paul leaned against the sink with his arms crossed over his chest and one leg crossed over the other, not touching the peach. I sat, tense and quiet, tracing a design in the table, then smoothing my hand over the surface as if to erase it.

"I'm not an idiot. I know how to drive," he said.

I looked at him sulking by the window and averted my eyes, unwilling to see how suddenly handsome he appeared in his jeans and T-shirt and his bad mood.

"You have no idea how much I hate being out of control," I said.

"I'm getting the picture, believe me." He bent down and plucked a slice of peach from the plate, slipped it in his mouth and sucked the juice from his fingers.

"I was in a car wreck," I said.

"When?"

"About a month ago."

"I wondered about those bruises around your eyes."

"Did you think I was a battered wife?"

He sat down across from me and took another slice. "Would you tell me if you were?"

"No." A surge of relief that was nearly happiness eased the tension in my face.

"I'd tell you if I was a battered wife," he said.

"I'm sorry I yelled at you," I said.

Paul turned his face up to catch another dripping slice in his mouth. He chewed, grinning. "There's just something so attractive about a woman apologizing to me."

"Any woman?" I stood up and turned on the faucet to wash my hands, then wiped the counter with a sponge, avoiding his eye.

"You in particular," Paul said.

Three

We'd been in Canyonlands for five days when the sky turned dark. Lightning glimmered on the horizon and a moody wind shoved against the walls of the Winnebago. Paul went off for a long hike in the afternoon and I stayed inside to read, but after reading the same sentence nine times in a row, I gave up and let my eyes wander over the interior of my RV.

When the previous owner pointed out all the hidden compartments in the Winnebago he claimed it could sleep six people, but I never figured out where to stow the table once it was unscrewed from its metal post. You had to remove it to make room for the sofa to pull out into a bed, and it looked like you'd have to be a dwarf to fit on it anyway. Maybe if you lined up four preschoolers head to toe on the floor you could find enough space for everybody to sleep, just so long as nobody needed to go to the bathroom in the middle of the night. It didn't matter; I was happy with the bed I had, and Paul seemed to like sleeping outside.

The dining table was crowded with Paul's souvenirs of the landscape, a tiny rabbit skull with teeth intact, cough syrup bottle that was at least sixty years old, rocks that Paul swore were fossils but no amount of squinting at them could make me believe it. His sneakers lined the narrow hallway by the closet-sized bathroom, and sixteen socks he'd washed the night before were draped over the side of the kitchen sink.

I felt a strange warmth looking at these traces of Paul, and realized I was grateful. Just a few days ago I'd missed Jake so much I felt as if I'd been shot in the chest. It had been about six hours since I'd even thought about Jake, and for me that was a new record.

When Paul finally came back I was happy to see him, and after dinner I even agreed to play chess with his pocket set. We cleared a space on the couch, sat down, and began to play. Paul liked to use his knights and I was slow at computing their crooked possibilities. In ten minutes I lost my queen. I muttered under my breath and tapped my forehead with a pawn.

"How old are you, Zoe?" Paul asked. I was in check, again.

"Why?"

He yawned without covering his mouth; the inside was puppy pink, and his teeth were white, unmarked by fillings. "Just wondered."

I felt myself bristle and moved my bishop. "Thirty-nine."

Paul slid his rook down to my king's row. "Old enough to know better. Check again."

"Where'd that money come from?" I said. I threw a balled up napkin at him; he caught it and flicked it back.

"God, you still don't believe me?" he said.

"Prove it."

Paul's eyes roved the interior of the Winnebago, as if he could pick evidence out of the air. His eyes settled on the cellular phone cradled between the front seats, and he bounced out of his seat to pick up the receiver. "Is this thing on?"

"No."

He flicked the switch, punched keys, and apparently got a dial tone in half the time it usually took me. After a few more stabs at the handset he paused to listen.

"Hi Dad," he said. A shock traveled through me that he would reach out and bring his father's presence into the space between us. Why would he call the man he'd been running away from since he was fourteen years old?

The side of the conversation that I could hear sounded normal and Paul seemed relaxed enough.

"I want you to meet my travel buddy," he said. "Her name's Zoe Harper, and she's a little suspicious about the money. Tell her I came by it honestly, okay? Here she is."

I glared at him as he held out the receiver to me. "Ask him," he said.

I held the phone to my ear. "Mr. Griffin?"

"Yes," a voice crackled in my ear. We both started talking at the same time, and then I shut up. "Where are you?" was the first coherent thing I heard him say.

"Utah."

"Is Paul all right?"

"Of course, yes, he's fine. We've been having a nice time," I said.

"Ask him," Paul said.

"Paul seems to be carrying a lot of cash. I wonder if you'd mind telling me where it came from?"

There was a longish pause. "Could I speak to my son for a moment?"

I held out the receiver and Paul took it.

"Yeah," he said. Another pause. "She's not like that," Paul said and listened to what must have been a lecture. "No. No. I have the money—"

I was beginning to feel like crawling into the wall. "No," Paul said heatedly. "No, goddamnit. No, I told you before, I'm not an idiot. I'm going to make my own decisions."

Finally he held the receiver out to me. "Here. Just talk to him."

"Hello," I said.

"Ms. Harper, I don't know what your relationship to my son happens to be, but it would be in your best interests to convince him to come back here before his actions reap some undesirable consequences."

"What actions?"

"I don't know what Paul has told you, but frankly I don't believe that the money he's carrying is any of your business."

I'd had enough. I held out the phone to Paul and listened with one ear to his half of the conversation while my thoughts curled in on themselves. Something odd was going on here, and Paul's father was not happy about it.

Paul said a few more words and hung up.

"Well?" he asked.

"Your father thinks I'm trying to nail you for your money."

Paul shrugged. "That's my dad."

"He said something about your actions reaping undesirable consequences."

"Sounds like him." Paul grinned.

"What's he do?"

"He's an investment analyst, city council member, on several boards for this and that. It drives him nuts that I'm dragging this much cash around."

"So where's the money come from? Him?"

"Indirectly."

"You lied about the lottery."

"Well. Yeah."

"This is so depressing," I said. I hated being lied to, and I hated his money.

"I'd tell you if I could," he said, and for a moment he looked wistful.

"Tell me, damn it!"

"Maybe tomorrow."

I snorted and tossed the chess board in his lap, all the pieces still fastened securely by their pegs to the board. Secrets infuriated me after living with Jake. Paul was too much of an unknown quantity, and his father was worse. My palms were suddenly damp.

I stood up and opened the refrigerator, found nothing I wanted and couldn't remember why I opened it. Paul put the chess set back on the table and eased out of his seat. As we both stood side by side I was freshly aware of his height as he looked down at me. His body filled the narrow aisle and I smelled his skin, different from the familiarity of my own. I took a step back. "How about a walk?" I asked.

"Sure," he said, reaching past my shoulder for his jacket. Paul's arm was close—did he know that? Was he testing me? I ducked under it, slipped out the door, and felt him follow. The storm hovered along the western horizon but the sky above us glittered with stars. My body relaxed as I walked. It was easier to breathe out here.

"Where were you born?" Paul's voice floated out on the black night, close beside me.

"Westport, Connecticut."

"Any brothers or sisters?"

"One. Marta. I'm on my way to San Francisco to stay with her. She lives with an AIDS widow, a sweet guy named Victor Lavett."

"Is she gay?"

"Sometimes. She's a performance artist, goes by the name of Z."

"Z is pretty minimal, for an artist."

"Her real name is Marta Harper, and a name like that could be a liability in her trade," I said.

"What does your dad do?"

"Advertising. Madison Avenue. He's a high roller, president of his own firm." Like Paul's father, mine believed in the power of money, and he was good at making it.

"Are you guys close?"

"No."

"Were you ever close?"

"When I was little." Richard had spoiled me then. Even before the canoe lessons, he'd let me carry his briefcase into my playhouse and fill it with modeling clay muffins. When I was young and sexless he was a tender father, but after I grew breasts he could hardly stand to look at me.

"So what's he like?" Paul asked.

"Vain. Elegant. Angry. He started drinking when I was about twelve. He worked harder, came home later. I think my mother makes him nervous."

"Why does your mom make him nervous?"

"She doesn't go out."

"She doesn't go out—ever?"

"She hasn't gone past her own front door in thirty years."

"How does she manage that?"

"You can get anything delivered, if you've got enough money. Even the church has a delivery service. Her priest comes to the house every

Sunday to say Mass, just for her. Religion is her only real indulgence."

"Valium of the masses," Paul said, and I was surprised at how smoothly he made the connection.

"Roman Catholic. Do they have deprogrammers for it yet? She writes prayers and types them up and sends them to me and my sister. Odes to the Virgin Mary, petitions to St. Francis. What was your mom like?" I asked.

"She died when I was little, so I don't remember her much. My dad took it hard. He was really distant when I was a kid. He'd come down for dinner, his nose in a book. No conversation from him or to him. It was like we lived on two different planets. I gave the poor guy nightmares for years. I was a bad little dude, always cutting school and hanging out with the worst kids I could find."

"Do you think you could ever be close?"

"We're too different to be close. He's a control freak, and I like to keep my options open. In his eyes I'm a failure. He doesn't care about what I want to do with my life."

"What do you want to do?"

"Beats me," Paul said.

"That's a broad field."

"I hate work."

"There must be something you want to do. What about cooking?"

"No way. I couldn't do it all the time, every day, year in and year out."

"What kind of jobs have you had?"

"I went back into the merchant marines after I busted out of college, worked as an able-bodied seaman for a couple years."

"Why did you quit?"

"Something happened."

"What?"

"We were on a run from New York to Lisbon, and this little guy who worked in the engine room was always complaining about the union. One night at dinner he tried to recruit a bunch of us into some kind of boycott. He wanted us to stop paying union dues."

"So?"

"He didn't show up for breakfast the next morning."

"What do you mean?"

"He was thrown overboard."

"Did he die?"

"We were several days out at sea. We didn't see him again."

I fell silent, digesting this.

Paul went on. "I cooked for some charter cruises around Barbados after that, but it gets old, feeding tourists who throw it all up anyway if the wind raises a ripple. I'm tired of working. Now I just want to go around and see things and meet people. If work is so important to you, why are you knocking around out here?"

"I'm older. I've had a career. I've made my money."

"What did you do?"

"Houses. I recycled them."

"You could make me a house," Paul said.

I glanced toward his face but couldn't read anything in it. I felt a flash of tenderness, as well as alarm that he would say such a thing. We walked along in silence, then paused to watch a shooting star streak through the eastern sky.

"Do you like being out here?" he asked.

I reached for his arm and held his elbow and gave it a little shake. "I like it a lot."

"So do you think I'm attractive?" Paul asked, bumping my side with his hip.

"Are you kidding?"

"No, no, I really want to know."

I grinned in the dark. "You have a really great personality."

Paul stopped walking. "You knucklehead," he said. "You take that back."

I ran ahead of him into the darkness, laughing. "Don't worry about it!" I called over my shoulder. "You're a real sweet guy!"

In the middle of the night the wind began to thrash the trees, whirling up dust and gravel that spattered against the side of the Winnebago. Darkness blotted out the stars and the air took on a new smell. Rain. The first big fat drops hit the dirt like wet bombs. Within seconds the sky opened up and poured slashing diagonal sheets of water onto the hard clay. Paul pounded on the locked door and shouted to rouse me.

I flicked on the light, clambered out of bed, shooed him inside, and tossed his drenched sleeping bag in the sink while he shrugged off his wet T-shirt and briefs. He looked shy and embarrassed as he bent over to grab a flannel shirt and sweat pants from his bag of clothes under the seat.

I glanced at his naked limbs, his tanned back, and the goose bumps on his pale buttocks. In college I'd taken a year of drawing classes and had seen plenty of male models, had drawn them for hours, but suddenly I felt awkward as a virgin. It had been a long time since I'd been anywhere near a naked man.

The rain was loud on the roof. I felt short of breath, uncomfortably aware of my body in its thin nightgown, and I climbed back into the loft, my face averted to give him privacy.

When I looked out the window to the storm, lightning touched the earth on the western horizon. A puff of smoke rose up as a tree caught fire and the smoke bloomed. Paul was dressed and drying his hair with a towel when I turned my face to him. The rain was still coursing down in sheets, the skies cracking and booming with thunder. The Winnebago enclosed us like a drum, vibrating with the clamor of the wind and rain, and I had to shout over the noise.

"Do you think we're okay under this tree?"

"I don't think we can move the camper in this," Paul yelled. "We'll be safer if we stay put."

I peered out the window. The dirt road had become a creek, covered with a flood of dark water that had risen six inches in as many minutes.

He tossed the towel over the back of the passenger seat and looked around for a place to go back to sleep. My books and clothes were strewn all over, and his collection of rocks and bleached bones were spread across the dining table. His eyes made a circuit of the interior and traveled back to my face. I shrugged, turned back the covers, and waited. Paul climbed up into the loft slowly, cautiously.

I turned off the light and we lay side by side in the small bed, not touching. I could smell his wet hair, a fragrance of lemon, probably his shampoo. His body radiated a heat that warmed the side of my leg and arm. It was a disconcerting sensation. The storm made sleep impossible, and talk was also out of the question. Every few seconds the RV was lit by a fork of lightning stabbing the ground nearby. Paul's face was brightly illuminated for a second or two, and then we were plunged into blackness again.

After a while the storm began to soften and the rain became a loose, sporadic handful of drops here and there. The clouds rolled on. From the loft I looked out at the stars, rinsed and glimmering. I opened the window a crack; the air smelled fresh and incomparably sweet.

"Paul—are you awake?" I whispered.

"Yeah."

"Do you ever think about getting old?"

"Why?"

"Sometimes I think about being eighty or ninety."

"Don't you think you're rushing it a little?"

"I don't want to be old, but the alternative isn't so great."

Paul laughed. "I want to die on a mountain before I get old."

"What do you think happens to us after we die?" I asked.

"I don't know."

"But what do you think?"

He turned on his side to face me, and I let myself relax a little next to the warmth of his body under the sheets.

"I think we'll see whatever we believe in. Like an atheist will believe he's dead and go into a coma. A Christian might see St. Peter. A Muslim might see Allah. I try not to believe in hell, myself."

"I bet we're going to be guided," I said.

"By what?"

"Oh, you know, guides. Go-betweens. I bet there are bus conductors on the other side. Or ferrymen. Whatever."

"You believe in angels?" Paul asked, his voice soft.

"I don't believe in angels that fly around playing the harp, but I believe in some intelligence out there that helps us."

"How?"

"By sending whatever . . . penetrates the bullshit. It might be a sudden sense of belonging, it might be money, or a job offer, or hope, or any strange gift that drops down on me from out of the blue. Like you."

There was a thick silence. I could hear him breathing, and my heartbeat quickened. He lifted his right hand and found my left hand, stroked my fingers with his fingers, threaded his fingers into mine until he held my hand securely against his palm.

"You're a very beautiful woman," he said. I squeezed his hand, then removed mine. My face was on fire.

"I won't do anything you don't want me to," Paul said into the cocoon of silence, "but I really would like to kiss you."

I was ashamed of the heat inside me and ashamed of my age. I was too old, I had seen too much to stain his life with my mistakes. The warmth of what could happen, might happen, would happen if I let it, fluttered against the wall of my better judgment. It was cold inside that wall but it was safe.

"I can't, Paul," I said. "You're too young."

Paul reached for my face and stroked it gently. "I'll stop if you really want me to," he whispered.

His mouth came close to my face. He kissed

my cheek, he kissed the corner of my mouth, softly, while I lay still under his caresses. It was almost cruel, how good it felt. Paul's lower lip fit the curve of my mouth and I couldn't stop myself from holding it for three seconds stolen from a week of flawless behavior. The way he kissed me was like being listened to. His breath lifted and sighed into me and our bodies curled around each other like snakes. My face tingled in the dark, and I knew I couldn't do this. I felt unbearably sad.

I turned away. "Stop," I said.

"Don't you like it?"

"That's not the point."

"Is this about the money? Or is it the age thing?"

"Yes."

"Pretend I'm fifty," he said, tracing my eyebrow with his finger. "Pretend I'm broke."

"No," I said. "I'm sorry. Look, I'll clear off the couch and sleep there if it's easier for you."

He stopped and lifted himself away from me, turned over, and held himself stiffly and politely apart, not touching me anywhere. Water dripped from the roof. It was the only sound, and I lay awake and listened to it for the rest of the night.

* * *

The next morning I pulled out the map of the western United States and examined the red route to Oakland, calculated the mileage, buttered my muffin across the table from Paul, and wouldn't meet his eyes. The light and hopeful bounce to his movements was extinguished. His eyes were flat and breakfast was silent. Packing was easy without any conversation to slow us down.

"Where do you want me to drop you off?" I asked.

"San Francisco," he said.

Fine, I thought, and didn't say another word.

An hour later I was still quiet as I drove through the desert terrain of the Great Basin. We crossed the Colorado Plateau, first north, then west across the Green River, toward Nevada. I-70 was a generic interstate, a bald, monotonous landscape that made my eyes restless. Eastern Nevada was ugly, the sky a dull mirror to the expanse of dirt and scrub. I felt as gray as the landscape.

Paul looked numb, hypnotized by the strobe effect of the utility poles as we went zipping by.

"Paul," I said, "I'd like to talk to you."

"Shoot," he said, not looking at me.

"I want to thank you for the week," I began awkwardly. "I really don't know what I would have done without you. But I want to spend some time by myself." I looked at the back of his head, his thick blonde hair caught in a braid that fell below his shoulder. "I need to go on alone."

No response. I was puzzled. I'd never been with a man who wasn't relieved to let me go. I assumed all men worshipped their freedom.

"What do you want, Paul?"

"I just want to stay a while."

"For another week? A month? A year?"

"I want to get to know you. What's so terrible about that?"

"That's just not enough."

Paul shrugged. "It is for me."

I looked out at the treeless plain. "I'll take you to San Francisco, if you like. You could visit your father. But then I think you need to find the right girl, the right life."

"Visit my father. Sure. Why not?" His voice was hard, sarcastic.

"You can do what you like," I said. "Just tell me how far you want to go."

"I want to go a lot further than you do."

"San Francisco?"

"Whatever."

I held my tongue. He was old enough to work it out. If he didn't want to go to his father's house, he could make some other arrangement. His problems had nothing to do with me.

"Maybe it's a sign," Paul mumbled, "this road being so boring."

The landscape changed toward late afternoon. The road climbed toward the Sierra Nevadas, trees appeared and thickened as we gained elevation and the air cooled noticeably. Paul slumped in the passenger seat and stared listlessly out the window, his face touching the glass. A thin snow began to fall, exasperating me as much as his silence. I threaded the pass and began the long descent, eager to be done with the slick and icy part of the journey.

We rolled into Placerville in the early evening. The snow had turned to drizzle, the gas gauge read empty, and I was stiff from driving. There was a carnival in town, and I could see a Ferris wheel turning, its candy colored lights bright in the darkness. I pulled into a gas station and prodded Paul.

"You want anything?"

"No."

The florescent glare and chatter of the store was a relief after so many hours on the road, trapped with Paul and his mood. My eyes were blurry from the strain of driving, my neck felt like iron, and my stomach was queasy from pistachio nuts and too many Cokes. For the first time in days I thought of Percodan, how great it would be to just pick up a bottle with gas and groceries. The clerk counted out my change. I struggled to fit the bills in my wallet, the coins in the zippered compartment of my purse.

After filling the tank with gas I put the pump back in its cradle and climbed back in the driver's seat. Paul was gone, probably to the restroom. A minute or two later I started the engine and moved the Winnebago to a vacant lot beside the store, turned off the engine, leaned back, and closed my eyes. Even with my eyes shut I could see the yellow stripes of the road spinning out ahead of me, a mirage of snowflakes swirling into my vision. Too tired to move, I listened to cars sizzle past on the wet pavement. Paul had been gone a long time.

I groaned and stepped out, walked up to the men's room and knocked on the door. An old man with a red plaid hunting cap stepped out and threw me a dirty look.

"Paul?" I called inside. No reply.

I ran into the store and paced down every aisle, searching.

"Did you see a young man come in, blonde,

long hair, wearing a green windbreaker, black jeans?"

The clerk shook his head and kept counting change. Three customers looked at me curiously but offered no help.

I stepped back out into the night and ran to the RV, opened the door and checked behind his seat: His duffel bag had disappeared. He was gone. I was astounded. I stomped back to the side door and slammed it shut behind me, then locked it with a hammerblow of my fist. My hands shook. A fresh anxiety seized me for my own safety, here in a strange place, alone.

I couldn't drive anymore. Taking off my shoes, I crawled into bed and pulled the covers over my face. This felt so familiar. It was just more divorce.

In the past two months I'd eaten at least a hundred meals alone. I'd learned to talk to myself when the isolation became too intense, and it was fine, I could do it for years if I had to. But all that solitude felt like marking time, as if I were a prisoner serving a life sentence, or an astronaut living on Tang and powdered eggs.

In my single past—fifteen years ago—I'd escaped loneliness by offering sex to whoever looked clean and charming and available, but now there was AIDS, and even if AIDS didn't exist there was too much sadness in me to offer it. The cliche of being dumped for a younger woman had frozen me. If anyone made love to me now it would melt ice in my heart I didn't want melted; it would take me down a river of sorrow and drown me. All I'd wanted from Paul was something navigable, like friendship, something where loss of control was not required.

When I woke up I thought it was still night until I saw the gunmetal gray light in the east, the first glimmer of dawn. I lay awake until the sun forced its way over the mountains, and then I got out of bed and dragged a comb through my hair. After pulling on jeans and a sweater I shouldered my purse, walked down the street, and ducked into a cafe. It was so crowded I lost heart and turned to go, when a busboy caught my eye as he cleaned a tiny table by a window in the corner. He waved his rag at me cheerily and pointed to the chair he had just wiped. I edged through the crowded tables and settled my coat and purse and sunglasses into the empty chair opposite. The ceilings were high and the windows were tall and wide; the white tiled floor held twenty tables full of people, and the clatter of plates and cups and glasses and voices and cutlery was loud.

The window was cold against my shoulder. I

ordered coffee from the waiter and looked out at the traffic on the street. The coffee came and I drank it. My eyes were still strained and tired, and I rubbed them as I mulled over my options.

"What's your name?" I asked when the waiter refilled my cup. I would meet people again, damn it.

He looked at me blankly. "Zack," he said. "Sorry ma'am, I'm kind of busy—gotta go."

Four

The fog curled around my ankles and the ocean pulsed beyond the pool of light where I stood pushing the button next to Marta's name. I could hear it buzz six times before her voice growled through the intercom. "What?"

"Is that how you answer your doorbell?"

"Zoe! Where are you?"

"Where do you think?"

"Fantastic! Come on up."

There are no words for the satisfaction of seeing your sister if she is the one person left on this planet you really love. Marta was wearing a cap of pink fake fur with bunny ears sewn on top that flopped as she looked me up and down. She looked great. Her whip thin body was sheathed in a leotard that revealed different bits of skin through strategically placed rips. Without saying a word she folded me into the kind of sisterly death grip that says you've been gone too long and I'm not letting you go until I strangle you a little.

"Here you go," she said, untying her cap of bunny ears. Her hair was shorter than I'd ever seen it, no more than half an inch, a canary yellow that would never appear in nature. "These will cheer you up."

I let her put the bunny ears on my head but refused to tie the strings under my chin. "I think these only work for you," I said.

She fluffed the ears out and said, "It's true, but it makes you more fun to look at. Come in, come in."

As she walked ahead of me into the apartment she told me her roommate, Victor, was away on a buying trip, which suited me because Victor took up a lot of space in the apartment even when he was out of town. The living room was crowded with dark furniture, swags of velvet drapes, chandeliers that could bonk your head and porcelain animals scattered over every available surface, including the floor.

Marta's room contained a futon on the floor and a crate turned over to make a table. There was an ashtray on it with a small heap of burnt feathers spilling over the sides. We sat on the futon with our backs against the wall. She held my hand, and I didn't mind.

"What's that?" I asked, tilting my head toward the ashtray.

"I've been reading about Jamaican curses," she said, "and I think I've figured out how to make Jake impotent."

"Good," I said. "Go for it."

"So how was your trip?"

"It started out tear-soaked and kind of boring but then I picked up this guy about a week ago."

Marta's hand tightened on mine. "What kind of a guy?"

"Young. Cute. His car broke down, he was hitchhiking. We spent a few days together in Canyonlands."

"I can't believe I'm hearing this! You traveled with a strange man? What's his name?"

"Paul Griffin."

"Did you fuck him?"

"No."

"Why not?"

"Too young. Eleven years too young."

"Hey, those young ones are energetic. Take advantage. You say he's cute?"

"He is."

"So what are you scared of? Sex is a good thing, Zoe, remember?"

"Easy for you to say."

"Pretend I'm your conscience. I approve. I deeply, deeply approve, and besides, think how much it would piss off Jake."

"Any word from the father-to-be? I gave him your address in case he needed to reach me."

"Yeah, the asshole sent you a letter from his lawyer. It's over there. They want to get married fast, I guess."

I started to cry. It was a relief to drop the pretense that I could handle everything.

Marta patted my hand as if it were a dying sparrow. "This is probably the worst thing that's ever happened to you, huh."

"No," I snuffled. "Living with our parents was worse."

"You have a point."

"How's Mom?" I asked, wiping my face with a corner of Marta's sheet.

"Who knows? I ask her how therapy is going—how do they afford this, anyway? The shrink is commuting from Manhattan for chrissakes—and she says fine. Then I ask her if she's gone out to get the mail yet and she says oh no, she's not that far along."

I perked up just thinking about my mother,

who is ten times more neurotic than either of us. "I don't think she wants to go out. The shrink is just window dressing, so we won't bug her about it."

"Where does this shit start? Gram never left the house either, not after her husband died," Marta said.

"They say it's a learned anxiety. A reaction to the threat of some dark, forbidden impulse coming out, so you avoid situations where it might pop up. Like I avoid living in Santa Fe because I might kill Jake."

"I think Mom was raped."

"No way. When? By whom?"

"It happens every ninety seconds in the United States," Marta said combatively.

I disengaged my hand from Marta's and plucked the bunny ears off my head. "I remember when she'd go out, before you were born. She'd go camping with us, or take me to the store, and it was never easy. She was always a wreck, she'd warn me a million times about snakes or muggers or getting my clothes dirty."

"God, I have no memory of her ever stepping outside the house," Marta said.

"My point is that she was always Gram's little girl, you know? She did everything just the way

Gram wanted her to. Gram was scared, so she was scared."

"Well, that's just sick."

"Mom didn't want to leave her mother. She never rebelled. I think she learned the phobia from her."

"We must be the healthiest kids who ever lived, if rebelling is healthy. I'll never forget the weekend I told them I was gay and you told them you were dropping out of law school to be an artist."

I smiled. "Mom was more pissed off at you than me."

"Yeah, right, Mom, the homophobe. The queen of unsolicited advice. That fucking busybody. She walked in on me and Nancy Corrigan, right after you called to give them the bad news."

"No kidding!" I said, "I never knew Nancy was gay."

"She's not. She was just curious."

"There was something else I don't think I ever told you," I said.

"What?"

"I was doing this geography report on South Africa when I was in sixth grade. Dad lent me some slides he'd taken there in sixty-two." Richard had thousands of slides from his travels and kept them in a cedar closet in his study, with insulated doors and a dehumidifier that ran constantly to protect the collection.

"Yeah? So?"

"So in the middle of all these pictures of Capetown, there were about six shots of Mrs. Rasmussen in a hotel room—"

"Dad's secretary?"

"And she was naked in every one of them . . ."

"Oh my God," Marta gasped, bursting into giggles. "She was a dog! Why would Dad go for her?"

"Opportunity, I guess . . ."

"So you think this has something to do with Mom being scared to go outside?"

"Well, I was only nine or ten when I saw those pictures. I was really shocked. Mom was outside weeding the garden—"

"Jeeze, I can't imagine her actually outside, weeding—"

"—She was wearing a dust mask, of course—"

"Right. Her 'allergies,' " Marta snorted.

"—so I ran to Mom and shoved these slides into her hands. And she took her gardening gloves off very carefully and held the slides up to the light, one by one. Then she thanked me for showing them to her."

"What a control queen," Marta said disgustedly. "I'd have decked you. Or him."

"Hey, thanks a lot—"

"So then what?"

"She picked up her trowel and dandelion fork and went inside. I don't think I ever saw her outside after that."

"So it's all your fault."

"Oh yeah, absolutely."

"In that case my therapist will send you her bill." Marta scrambled off the bed and into the bathroom to search for her Pall Malls. When she found them I could hear the scratch of the match, the suck of her inhale through the open door.

"I've missed you, M. Are you working tonight?"

"You bet," Marta said, exhaling. She leaned against the doorway and sent out a plume of smoke. "We got a gig at Club Luna. I have to be there at ten, but that'll give us at least an hour to catch up. You could come and see our new show if you want."

"Will I hate it?"

"Yeah, probably. This one is shrill, lots of dissonance."

"Can we drive over there in my Winnebago? I parked it outside in a loading zone."

Marta grabbed a handbag that could easily hold a week's worth of laundry from the hook on the bathroom door and threw her cigarette in the toilet. "You better pray it's still there."

The Winnebago was filthy and I was proud of it. It looked like I'd been somewhere, done something. I unlocked the side door and ushered Marta into the living quarters.

"Doesn't it feel like you're driving a semi?" she asked.

"It's the smallest model they make. Power steering, power brakes, power everything."

"This is like something out of the fifties," Marta said. "The mobile retirement home." She sat on the couch and bounced, testing it, frowning. "You're too young to drive this thing."

She's worried about me, I thought, surprised, and I watched her as she rose from the couch to peer in the bathroom and run her fingers over the sink and four-burner stove. I waited while Marta poked the numbers on the microwave.

"Don't you miss your house?" she asked.

"I try not to think about it."

"I got a call from your realtor," Marta said. "Some guy who works at Los Alamos made an offer. She thinks you should take it."

"Then I guess I will."

"Zoe, you're scaring me. That house is your baby."

"Not anymore. It's been on the market for a month."

"There's a tow truck coming," Marta said, peering through the window into the side mirror. "Let's get this monster moving."

I hopped behind the wheel, pulled away from the curb, and had the pleasure of seeing the tow truck hit the lights and then turn them off, as if it had inadvertently burped.

"Oh my God," Marta said, flinging one arm over the back of her seat to watch the cupboards sway with each pothole. "This thing is huge."

"That's why I bought it."

"I must say you look suspiciously healthy. Are you sure you didn't fuck this guy?"

"Positive."

"He was just too young and gorgeous, huh?" Marta dipped into her purse for a cigarette. "Got a match?"

"Probably in the back, in the silverware drawer."

"How about the glove compartment?" She clicked it open and a crumpled paper bag fell out at her feet. It looked familiar, but it took me a second to remember what it held.

"Holy shit," Marta said, looking inside.

* * *

I phoned Paul's father from the parking lot outside Club Luna. There were only three Griffins listed in Petaluma, and I got his voice on my second try.

"Your son left some money in my RV," I said.

"Thank you for letting me know," he said, as if he were used to hearing this sort of thing. "I was afraid something like this might happen."

"I want to return it."

"Certainly. Are you nearby? I could arrange to have a messenger pick it up, if you like."

"I'm not sure how long I'll be here. I'd rather drop it off. Do you have an office in San Francisco?"

"No, I work out of my home. It's about an hour north of the city."

"Could I have the address?"

He hesitated, as if he were doing me an enormous favor. "1212 Fairmont Road."

"I'll be there tomorrow morning."

After I disconnected, Marta took a quick drag off her cigarette to hide a smile. "So is the little prince going to be there?"

"None of your beeswax."

"Is he rich and careless about where he leaves his money? That's a lovely combination."

"This particular chunk of money makes me

nervous. The little creep never did tell me how he got it, but his dad seems to know all about it."

"Let me come with you to his dad's," Marta said.

"Why?"

"Maybe they'd like to make a donation to the arts."

"Not on your life."

"One look at this boy will let me know how much trouble you're in," she said.

"No trouble at all, M. Thanks but no thanks."

The club looked like a warehouse, windowless and painted black inside and out. I followed Marta through the door and into a darkness so complete it took me a few seconds to see her outline next to me. I grabbed her sleeve and trailed after her, and as my sight returned I could see a few technicians dressed in black, taping wires to the stage. Marta led me to a corridor lined with racks of costumes and closed doors. She opened one of the doors, flicked on the lights, and pushed me ahead of her into a dressing room as narrow as the hallway, with one large illuminated mirror and a counter in front of it.

Marta sat in front of the mirror and stared at

her face as if it were land that could be developed. I perched on a padded armchair that smelled like cat piss and watched her slip a white stretch band from her purse around her head.

"First, pancake." She opened a flat jar and sponged her face with a paste that made her face look as if it had been dipped in white paint.

Laughter and footsteps approached until five women filled the doorway and flowed around me to seat themselves in front of the mirror. Only one of them looked familiar from the last performance I'd seen, but I couldn't remember her name. They greeted Marta and cast speculative looks at me.

"She's my sister, and she's straight," Marta said, "so let's show a little respect."

"Hey babe." The tallest one bent to kiss Marta and gave me a good view of her crewcut, which was the color of spring lettuce.

Marta looked happy and foolish, the way people do when you've caught them in the act of falling in love. "This is Zoe," she said. "Meet Roberta."

"Hi," I said.

Roberta left one hand on Marta's shoulder and squeezed it possessively. "So you're Zoe."

"So you're Roberta." I didn't like her. She

looked like a Nazi in her black leather jacket. And then there was the hair.

"It's freezing in here," Marta said. "Somebody go see if we can get some heat. Jo, do you have any more of that Cappuccino lip gloss?"

"Don't forget to give it back," Jo said, handing it to her. "Like last time."

"You wound me," Marta said, buttering her lips with the lipstick. "Zoe, would you be a doll and see about the heat? And bring me some coffee. The bartender probably has a pot going."

I was glad to have an excuse. Maybe Marta knew that, or maybe she was just being her usual bossy self. "Bye-bye, Zoe," the rest of them caroled in schoolgirl sing-song as I slid out the door.

By the time the show began there were at least three hundred people crammed around tiny little tables and lined up six deep at the bar. For the past week I'd been going to bed at ten, waking up at six. Now it was close to midnight, my eyelids felt grainy, and I couldn't stop yawning. There was an hour and a half of loud music from the opening act to sit through before Marta's group hit the stage, and I had to stuff pieces of cocktail napkins in my ears to dim the auditory assault.

But there is something electrifying about watching your sister walk onstage stark naked, wearing a pair of dirty pink bunny ears on her head. I took a deep breath and forgot to let it out for a few seconds. I wished she didn't have to do it naked. She was thirty years old and she looked excruciatingly vulnerable up there, more naked than a Playboy model or a porno star. Her ribs were visible. Her pubic hair was black. Marta stood between Jo and another woman and they were all naked except for a Raggedy Ann doll tied to Jo's back and the other woman had a muzzle strapped to her face.

The rest of the troupe came out. Each one was covered by a white tube that rose from the ankles and snaked up seven or eight feet in the air like a slinky. One white slinky woman—Roberta, no doubt—went to Marta and lowered the top end of her slinky over my sister's head. Marta's body shook as it was engulfed by the tube, which bulged in a weird imitation of feeding or rape, I wasn't sure which. And then Marta lifted the tube from Roberta's body until Roberta was revealed, also naked, and her face was painted like a clock. The other dancers repeated this motion of devouring and being devoured while a dialogue of amplified grunts and shrieks and whistles expressed their love-hate relationship at a pitch designed to make me glad I'd already filled my ears with napkin. None of it was erotic.

Like all of Marta's shows, it made me extremely uncomfortable, but her performances rarely lasted more than forty minutes, which I always thought was one of the best things about them. The audience was with her, they were riveted and silent and I was proud of her for that.

As I watched the stage I could see that she'd gotten something right about humans who connect and then immediately have to see who can eat the other up.

The dyads on stage became less frenzied and began to moo in long low tones that formed an eerie harmony. The tubes were shared, disguising all but their feet, and their movements became slow and collaborative as they formed a procession of pairs walking in cadence.

Suddenly I was ripped by an unexpected sadness, and I wanted to swim away from the crowd and out of the room before it spilled out of me. I wanted to run across the parking lot to the RV, unlock the door and relock it behind me, throw myself down on the couch and pull a pillow over my head. My breath was coming in short gasps and I felt something trying to claw its way out of me, and I knew I didn't want it to come out here. Not just here, in the nightclub, but here, in San Francisco, with Marta to witness it. I didn't want her seeing me like this. I wanted to go to some empty place where I could fall apart in peace and no one would know me.

Backstage, after the show, they were riding high on applause and adrenaline.

"Come on out with us," Marta said to me. "Let's get really drunk and dance all night. Roberta's dying to get to know you."

"I'm dead, M. I've got to crash."

"Are you sure?"

"I've never been so sure."

"Okay, let me find the keys to the apartment. If Victor's back just tell him I'll probably be at Roberta's tonight. You can sleep in my bed—there are clean sheets in the bathroom closet."

"Marta, forget it. I have my bedroom out there in the RV. I'm used to it. I'm not going to pack a bag just to spend one night in a strange bed."

"What do you mean, just one night? I thought you were going to stay for a week."

"No, I'm going to head out tomorrow."

She was pissed. "How long do you think you can go on running away?"

"As long as I want."

"Why can't you run away here," she whined.

"I'll see you on my way back."

"You're a shit, Zoe," she said, clutching me to her neck. "I really hate you sometimes."

"I know," I said. "Sometimes I hate me too."

I drove to Ocean Beach, which was the nearest access to the Pacific. There was a parking lot overlooking the water, and I pulled in close to the flat gray stretch of sand. Dark cliffs loomed at each end, and the scattered rocks below the cliffs were covered with sleeping sea lions. I smelled a charcoal fire burning down the beach, smoke mixed with the tang of salt air, rising above the deeper chill coming from the water.

I lit half a dozen candles and placed them around my loft, made a cup of mint tea and lay propped up on pillows in bed while I watched the moon dip toward the Pacific. The light cut through the glossy swale of a cresting wave and shadows of kelp rose and fell within it. I sipped my tea. The sound of the ocean booming against the sand was steady as a heartbeat. It was colder now, and I was so tired I couldn't keep my head up. I put my teacup on the shelf by my pillow and let the candles gutter down to puddles as I dozed off in the nutshell of my motor home, this box I'd tucked myself into, out of harm's way.

In the morning I woke up too early and drank too many cups of coffee and spent the resulting jitters gassing up the Winnebago and restoring its vital fluids. Then I washed it with a bubble brush, polished the windows inside and out and used up four dollars in quarters vacuuming the interior. I spent another hour doing the dishes, putting away all my clothes and books, and throwing Paul's rocks and bones and money in a cardboard box.

By ten I was on the road to Petaluma. Beyond the urban congestion of the coast and just a few miles inland, the farms began. The fog had cleared off, revealing blue sky. Soft mounds of hills covered with green grass rippled in the wind, as if invisible hands were stroking their curves. Live oaks dotted the hills, their branches low and heavy, while a scattering of cows worked the fields with their heads down. There were dozens of newborn calves and lambs and foals in the farmland I passed through. It was spring.

After taking the turnoff for Petaluma, I stopped at a vegetable stand to ask directions to Fairmont Road and was told I was only a mile away. I drove slowly past the gentrified downtown and came to a clearly marked lane that ran between wide fields dotted with ranch houses built in the fifties.

Pastures flanked both sides of the road, with a sprinkling of cows on either side, heads down in the green. I was barely moving, studying addresses on a group of mailboxes when a cow pie landed on the windshield and stuck to it like a wet brown kiss.

"Son of a bitch," I said and braked to a halt on the deserted road. I opened the door, stepped out, and saw Paul scramble up the side of a culvert, dragging his duffel bag. "What the hell are you doing?" I asked.

He looked terrible. There were scratches on his face and mud and straw in his hair and on his clothes. He ran to the passenger door and jumped in, ducking down in the seat as if terrorists were after him.

I plucked the cow pie off the windshield and climbed back into the cab. "Please," he whispered. "Get me out of here."

"What's wrong? Why are you out here? Why aren't you at your dad's house?"

"Will you help me or not?"

"How can I help if I don't know what's wrong?" But I turned the Winnebago into a driveway and backed out slowly. I flicked a look at his face and saw a bruise next to his left eye.

"Move!" he squeaked, still trying to whisper.

"I'm moving. Now talk to me."

But Paul didn't speak for at least a minute, not until I was back on the highway and headed away from Fairmont Road. His arms were tightly crossed against his chest, his shoulders hunched as if he were in pain.

"Thanks," he said, finally.

"What happened?"

"He told me he was going to make me get a job. For my own good, he kept saying. He said he was sick of watching me ruin my life and waste the resources I'd been given. He said I needed the discipline of a career and if I couldn't make that happen then he'd have to do something."

Just looking at Paul made me hate his father. I'd never seen him look tentative or uncertain, and now he looked afraid. "How'd you get that black eye?"

"We were arguing. He pushed me. I tripped on the rug and my head caught the corner of the coffee table. After that I ran out and spent the night by the road to wait for you. He told me you'd probably never show up, but I knew you would."

"Will he look for you?"

"I don't see how. Last night he couldn't even remember your name. 'That woman,' he called you. He was really pissed I left my money in here."

"Why did you leave it?"

Paul raked his fingers through his hair. "I don't know. It was before that last day. I got tired of moving that bag out of the way every time I wanted clean clothes, so I stashed it up front. I just forgot it."

"Paul, I have to know. Tell me where you got the money."

Paul took in a breath and let out a little sigh. "I sort of took it."

Somehow I was not surprised. "From?"

"My dad sent me to pick up a package from a developer who wants permission to drain a hundred acres of marsh."

"Why would a developer be sending a package to your dad?"

"My dad's on the Land Planning Commission for the county. They make recommendations to the zoning board and the zoning board rubber-stamps their decisions pretty much down the line. It's a very cozy political scene here."

"And this was a bribe? The package had a hundred thousand dollars in it?"

"No."

"No?"

"It had two hundred thousand in it."

I was nodding and driving along as if I were having a perfectly normal conversation with a nice-looking young man who wasn't a felon. "So you stole two hundred thousand dollars," I said, helping him along with the story, my voice just as calm as any brain-dead getaway driver's would be, and all the while I'm praying that he'll start laughing and then I'd laugh and we'd go on to the next topic.

He shrugged and gave me a miserable smile. "Yeah."

"Are you crazy? Do you think they'll just let it go?"

"No."

"You have to give it back."

"I know."

"They could be coming after you with a serious attitude, not to mention warrants and sheriffs and sworn complaints."

"My dad never told anybody I took the money. He's stalling them. And it's not exactly legal, forking out bribe money to elected officials."

"How long can he go on stalling?"

"I don't know. It depresses me to think about it."

"Why did you do it?"

"I grew up next to that marsh. It's beautiful. Great bird habitat. But to tell you the truth I did it mostly to fuck with my dad's head. Ever since I dropped out of college he's been grooming me to be some kind of errand boy. Like I should be really grateful to run around town kissing his ass and picking up bribes."

"Where's the rest of the money?"

"I buried it."

This was getting too bizarre for me. "Where exactly did you bury it?"

"Montana," he said. "I drove there right after I took the money. I just wanted to disappear for a while."

"When did you do all this?"

"A few weeks ago, right before I went down to Arizona and met you."

"You have to give it back," I repeated. I held on to this thought like a life preserver.

Paul slumped in his seat and I was sorry I'd said anything. He looked exhausted. "It's in a safe spot. Right now I just want to get out of California."

"We can do that," I said.

Five

I told Paul to wash his face and take a nap in the back while I drove. The Winnebago was gaining some elevation, and the grass had given way to chaparral and scrub oak. Outside the window I could see mountains still capped with snow, held fast by the lock of winter. The steady rise of the highway brought us to the high tundra of Donner Pass, where patches of old snow were melting in the May sunshine. The ground still wore the drab colors of winter—buckskin browns and the bleached tan of last year's grass. We passed over the spine of the Sierras and coasted down toward Nevada.

I took a deep breath when we crossed the state line, inhaling the smell of Paul in my space, the scent of his soap and something deeper, sweat on skin, a whiff of locker room. What he'd told me about his father and the money twisted in my mind as I mused over his story. Paul could be lying. He'd already lied about the lottery. Except he was carrying all that cash, and where did it come from if he didn't steal it? Why would he lie about stealing it? Maybe Paul was telling the truth and he had just pissed off some very powerful and unscrupulous people. They might soften their reaction because he was related to one of them, but it seemed unlikely Paul's father would have any tender feelings of forgiveness for me.

I've never cheated on my income tax. Whenever a cashier hands me too much change I give it back. There are a million ethical corners you can cut in the building trade, but I never cut one of them. This painstaking honesty is not due so much to my upbringing but to something that happened to me almost thirty years ago, in high school.

Pamela Fox and I were shopping for bathing suits in Holley's Department store one afternoon. Pamela's parents were richer than God and she probably had enough money in her wallet to buy a small sports car, but that day I saw her sweep a bottle of nail polish off the cosmetics counter and into her purse. Then she winked at me.

I was dumbfounded. It had never occurred to

me to steal anything from a store. This seemed like a lack of imagination on my part, so I tried it. I took three swimsuits into the dressing room and tried on one of them. It fit okay. It wasn't the sort of thing I'd usually buy, it was a little more daring and low cut than most of my sixteen-year-old friends' bathing suits, but it turned out to be the first, last, and only thing I ever decided to steal.

I put my clothes back on over the swimsuit and returned the other two to the rack. Who would know? In those days, and in that store, there was no clerk to count the items we'd taken into the dressing room. But when I tried to leave the store a large detective stepped in front of me and said, "Aren't you forgetting something?" Pamela kept right on walking, and I didn't see her again for a week.

A female clerk took me back to the dressing room and I was instructed to take off my clothes in front of her. When she saw the bathing suit, price tags still dangling, she smiled. It was a vicious smile. The police were called and they brought me down to the station, where I was photographed and fingerprinted. Then I had to call my father and wait in a jail cell for him to come and bail me out, and he let me wait a long time.

That experience taught me two things: one, dressing rooms are outfitted with two way mirrors and/or hidden cameras, and two, I shall not steal, not ever, ever again.

So it was absolutely clear to me what had to be done. I exited the highway and pulled into the nearly empty parking lot of a strip mall. Under the fluttering state flag of Nevada a tiny post office was wedged in between the other storefronts. I came to a halt in front of it, turned off the ignition, and opened the glove compartment. The bag was still there. I took it out, unrolled the top and looked at the cash inside. Then I re-rolled it, tucked it under my arm, and went back to talk to Paul.

He was lying in a fetal curl on the couch, eyelids slack with sleep. I shook him awake.

"If you want to go any farther with me you have to return this to your dad." I thrust the bag into his hands.

His face was blank, but he took the bag. "Uh-huh."

"We're in Nevada. At a post office. I want you to go in there and mail this back to him, registered, certified, express, overnight, priority."

"I get the picture," he said, and knuckled the sleep out of one eye.

"You're okay with this?"

He tightened the corners of his mouth and looked away. "No."

"At least it'll show your good intentions. Write him a note, say you'll send back the rest, too."

"And if I don't send it back?"

"You get out here. End of ride."

"I need a pen," he said, and sat up and reached for his shoes.

I found a pen and notepad in the glove compartment and brought them back to him. Paul scrawled a note that I shamelessly read over his shoulder: "Returning this to you—will send the rest in a week. Paul." He tore off the sheet, tucked it into the bag, and looked relieved. "Okay, let's do it," he said.

The clerk at the counter looked happy to see us, glad for a diversion in the midmorning slump. "Yes, ma'am," she chirped, assuming I was in charge.

I put my hand on the small of his back and shoved Paul forward.

"I need a padded envelope big enough to hold this," he said, and held up the bag.

The clerk eyed the bag and reached under the counter for an envelope lined with bubble wrap. Paul wrote his father's address on it twice—under TO and FROM—then slid the bag inside.

"Registered and certified," I said.

A flicker of a smile crossed Paul's face. The clerk weighed it and gave Paul a slip of paper to fill out. Then the package was stamped, sealed, stapled, and thrown in a bin by the wall.

"Thanks," Paul said after I paid and pocketed the change. He held the door for me and when we came back into the sunny day of the parking lot I felt as if a pile of bricks had been lifted off my back. That damn money had plagued me for weeks, sent me miles out of my way, and yanked me from my plans again and again. Now it was finally gone.

"Feel better?" Paul asked. He smirked at me as if my conscience showed a lack of nerve, a caution he was too young to understand. He was the one who didn't understand. I've been this way since I was sixteen and had to spend five hours in jail waiting for my father to show up.

"I feel better," I admitted. "Maybe I'll even let you drive."

Paul's face looked like the sunrise, delight breaking across his features as he held out his hand for the keys. My eyes held his as I continued to swing the keys above his open palm.

"On one condition," I continued.

He made a wry face and waited, hand out.

"You stop at each and every stop sign." My enunciation was crisp.

He shook his head. "And here I thought we were making so much progress on these control issues."

"I want you to take it easy, Paul."

He flashed me a smile. "No dragging on the strip with the other Winnebagos?"

"Take these before I change my mind," I said and dropped the keys into his hand.

"Where are we going?"

It was the obvious question. "If we go to Montana, will you swear to me you'll get the rest of the money and send it back to your father?"

I saw him take it in, what I was willing to do, what he might not be so willing to do. "I'll make you a deal," he said. "We get to where the money is and I'll let you decide what I should do with it."

"I won't change my mind."

"Deal?"

I shrugged. "Deal."

"You sure you're up for this?"

"No," I said.

"Don't worry. You're gonna love it," he said.

There were clean sheets on the bed in the loft, the dishes were all washed and put away, and the refrigerator was stocked with food. It smelled like Windex and cleanser in the cabin as we rolled northeast on I-80. I climbed into the loft and settled back to watch the changing view.

It felt strange to be chauffeured, to read or eat or stare out the window without bothering to watch the road. My body sagged on the pillows. The muffled voice of the radio was barely audible in the cab below me. I couldn't make out the words, but the drone of voices was comforting. For the last week I'd been alert, tense, ready to defend myself. Now I was so tired I couldn't keep my eyes open. My lids fluttered shut and I slept.

When I woke up I felt a queasy sadness, a dark undertow of bad feeling that floated without visible cause right below the surface of my skin. Paul was singing off-key along with the radio. His voice was too happy, and it grated on me. Wasn't he in too much trouble to be singing?

Maybe it was wrong to take Paul with me. Maybe I was too weak for solitude, although I'd always thought I had a knack for it. Something isn't right, a nagging, fretful voice inside me whined. Where is your husband? Why don't you have a child? The company of a stranger is a cheap imitation of what you miss. Sometimes the voice in the bleak center of my loneliness sounded exactly like my mother.

On the morning of my first wedding anniversary, I stood in the bathroom staring at the stick from the home pregnancy test kit. It was blue. I closed my eyes and opened them. It was still blue.

I threw the kit in the wastebasket, as if the pregnancy could be wiped from my body by getting rid of that stick of blue evidence. This was not the time for a baby, not with our new house being built. Our expenses were already beyond anything we'd anticipated, and we struggled from week to week under a crushing load of debt and unforeseen costs. My third house had been on the market for six months and there was still no buyer in sight. I wanted to save more money before I had a baby. If I ever had a baby.

Jake and I had never seriously talked about babies. Whenever I made requests of Jake that he didn't care to fulfill, his voice became chilly and he sulked for hours behind a freezing courtesy. His pleasure in my company was the fragile thread that bound us together, and I lived in fear of stretching it too far.

When we were dating I brought up the subject of parenthood once. I studied his face, watching for the telltale flicker of annoyance that might signal his withdrawal into coldness. The smile had frozen on his face. I knew what that meant. It meant "back off," and I did. It was always a delicate matter, bringing up a subject that might mean curtailing his freedom. Of course, children were a distant possibility, if I were very, very good. If I could show him that I'd take care of everything. When the time was right I would convince him.

"Are you done in here?" Jake asked, pushing the door open. He stood in the doorway in his pajamas, looking sleepy and vulnerable. My heart ached as I looked at him. He was so handsome. He smelled wonderful, even in the morning. We could have a gorgeous child together.

"I'm pregnant," I said.

He sat down heavily on the closed lid of the toilet.

"Damn," he said.

I felt a thudding disappointment. Tears gathered in the corners of my eyes. "I know. I'm not thrilled about this, either."

"You'll have to get an abortion."

"I'll handle it," I said. I studied my sweating palms, felt the rising nausea that meant life. Life.

The Greek word for life was Zoe. There was life inside me now but I wanted it dead.

Even now, years later, the abortion is still so sharp in my memory that I can only think about it in glimpses. Thinking about it at all is like holding razor-edged splinters of glass in my hand, and if I turn an image in my mind too long, it cuts.

"Looks like you're about nine weeks along," the doctor had said, administering Valium intravenously. I lay on the table with my feet up on the metal stirrups, my mind drifting into a false feel-good stupor, my bones turning to jelly. How easy it was. I could sense how much everyone wanted me to stay calm, to be brave, to shut up and let them do the thing they were being paid to do. There was a tug inside my womb, a soft sucking pull followed by a wave of cramps made distant by the Valium.

The doctor murmured to the nurse. Forceps clinked in a metal bowl. Deep in my drugged body a voice cried "No!" and I knew it was my baby's voice, a voice that wanted me. I knew it was a boy. It staggered me, the force of that voice, how particular and individual it was, and even though I had never heard it before, I recognized it and knew I would never forget it. The nurses whispered over the sound of running water in the sink while I lay on the table and wept.

On the way home from the abortion I knew I would leave Jake. He drove the car slowly, avoided every pothole and took the switchback turn to our driveway with oozing care. He carried me into the house. Neither one of us spoke. He wrapped me in a blanket, settled me on the couch, and went off to the kitchen to make me a tuna fish sandwich.

He fed me the sandwich bite by bite while I lay quietly chewing. This is the last time I will ever eat with this man, I thought. When he kissed my cheek I turned my face to the wall. I made a list in my mind of what I would take with me. Clothes. Jewelry. Photo albums. Marta would let me stay with her until I found a place of my own. It was too bad about the house, but the house wasn't that important after all.

The next day I slept very late, and when I woke up I took a Valium and started to pack. Jake came home at noon to check up on me.

"What are you doing?" he asked. We stood in the bedroom, the bed between us, my suitcase open on the bed.

I folded a sweater and put it in the suitcase. "I'm leaving."

"Oh, no," he said. "You're not leaving."

"I don't want to talk to you," I said.

"Please. Let me make it up to you. We can take a little trip."

"Go back to work. I don't want to look at you."

Jake came closer. If I weren't already dead inside I might have been afraid. But there was nothing he could do to make me feel worse.

"Zoe, you're not thinking clearly. You need to lie down for at least another day. If you want to leave tomorrow, go ahead."

I shook my head, walked into the closet, lifted a garment bag from the rod, and carried it to the bed. When I went back for my skirts, he followed me. We stood between the racks of clothing, mine on one side, his on the other.

"I can't let you go, Zoe."

"You don't have a choice."

"Everything will look different tomorrow."

"I'm sure it will," I said, slinging skirts over my arm.

"Don't go."

"Get out of my way."

"No." His face was reddening.

"What are you going to do? Lock me up?"

"That's not what I want," Jake said. And for the first time I understood that this was in fact exactly what he wanted, a wife who stayed in a very small space and didn't cause him any trouble.

"Then you'll have to let me go," I said, as if I were still in control. The closet seemed unbearably small.

He pushed me then, back into the soft layers of all the clothes we weren't wearing, and falling was a simple matter of leverage, upper body strength versus a lower center of gravity. I fell on my shoes and thought, Oh, shoes, I'll need to bring shoes. The closet door slammed and I felt the breath of air from its closing, heard the click of the lock.

I yelled for a few minutes, knowing no one could hear me who would help. I cried. I fell asleep and woke up in the dark. I could have been in there for hours or twenty minutes. Jake came back and let me out.

"Look what I brought you," he said, and gave me a bouquet of roses, so red they were almost black.

"I'm bleeding," I said, dropping the roses on the carpet. "There's blood all over the shoes."

I walked into the bathroom and sponged the blood off my thighs. The doctor had told me to expect this. It was all right.

The center of my body was freezing. The apricot tree outside the bathroom window was bare, and for a moment I couldn't remember if it were spring or fall, if plants had just died or were just coming back to life.

A week passed before I felt strong enough to leave Jake, and by then my practical nature had reasserted itself and divided the blame more evenly. There was no way I could have guessed how heavy this self-despising grief would be. Jake didn't feel it, but none of this was his fault. It was my fault. For months afterward I woke up in the middle of every night, aching for my baby.

Paul and I stopped for the night near Elko, in the mountains between the Independence and Cortez Ranges, a few miles from Emigrant Pass. The aspen were just turning green in the higher draws, and ponderosa pines cast long shadows over the chokecherry and mountain mahogany. It had been hot during the day when we were crossing the plains, but in the mountains the air cooled off quickly. I shivered as I stepped out of the RV to stretch and explore the campsite. The scent of vanilla from the ponderosas made me lift my head in pleasure as I buttoned my jacket. The sky was pink as coral.

We were parked near the top of a dirt road that meandered up a slow rise and gave out to a view of a town in the distance. A few lights glittered far off in the dusk. The tops of the cottonwoods below were just coming into leaf; spring had crept into the valley and hovered in the trees like green smoke. The ground was cushioned with pine needles, and I heard the clicking of stones in a nearby creek.

Paul emerged from the Winnebago to look around and shake off the hours of driving.

"So what's for dinner?" I asked.

"Damned if I know," Paul said absently, scratching his elbow.

"I wonder what kind of trees these are," I said, looking up at the dark branches.

"I might braise some chicken with your apricot jam."

I smiled. "When did you find that jam?"

"First time I ever cooked for you. Did you make it yourself?"

"Last year's harvest. In another time, another place, I actually used to cook." I wasn't really hungry yet. "I'm going to take a walk first."

"Take a flashlight," he said. "It's getting dark fast."

I pulled a pocket flashlight out of the glove compartment, switched it on, and wandered off through the trees toward the sound of the creek.

After a few minutes I came to a small clearing.

The sound of water was louder now, and I climbed an outcropping of granite to see the moon rise. The moon was the color of a pumpkin, bright gold-red and immense, lifting into the sky like a balloon filled with helium. It was a relief to be alone, after a day of being with Paul. Without his presence I felt lighter, looser, and I stretched my arms above my head to touch the extra space around me.

Each tree breathed out a coolness as I walked between the thick trunks and watched the moon appear and disappear in the canopy. Darkness stained the forest like ink spilled in water, and the first stars glimmered above the black tips of the firs.

Behind a mass of brambles I could hear a waterfall knocking against loose rocks. I kept my hands in my pockets and pushed through the shoulder-high briars to the flat rocks beside the stream. The waterfall was as tall as I was, pouring itself into a black pool. I knelt and put my hand in the water. It was like liquid ice, as cold as water could be and still run without freezing. When I took my hand out, the skin burned.

I stared at the shiny black water. There might be slime on the bottom, rotten corpses of frogs or trout, but the dark surface drew me in. I wanted to feel the liquid pain of it around me.

Slowly, reluctantly, I took off my jacket and unbuttoned my shirt.

The wind carried a thread of spray from the falls and the scattering of cold drops raised goose bumps on my arms. I unhooked my bra and let it fall from my shoulders. My fingers slid under the waistband of my underpants and I tugged them down my legs with my jeans. Finally I stepped out of the crumpled heap of my clothing as if I were sleepwalking. When my toes encountered the water I sucked my breath in a quick, involuntary gasp.

It took at least a minute to wade in up to my knees, every step a punishment. My feet were numb as iron. I shuffled forward, feeling along the slick bottom for a purchase on the rocks until I came to a dropoff.

Go, I told myself.

With a panicked yelp I plunged into the center of the pool, emerging under the freezing force of the waterfall. The icy water pounded my head, seized the last bit of warmth from my body, and tore it away. "Oh god oh god oh god," I spluttered. You could die doing this. It was agony. It was intolerable. It was fun. I floundered back to the ledge, whooping. My toes banged against the rock shelf and I clambered out, panting from shock.

I swore out loud and jogged in place to warm myself, shivering in the wind as I buttoned my shirt with fingers made clumsy with cold. My skin ached and then rippled with a tingling, silky, quick-blooded thrill of pleasure. My hair would be dripping wet when I got back to the campsite. Paul would be amazed. The anticipation of his amazement made me laugh out loud, gleeful as a child. I was wide awake and ravenous.

Hopping on one foot, I was about to pull on my sock when the bushes behind me rustled.

I let the sock dangle. Nothing moved.

"Who's there?" I called, making my voice gruff and threatening. Then I felt foolish—it had to be Paul. "Paul?" I asked the shadows. "Is that you?"

Silence, then a furtive crackle.

"You're not funny, Paul," I said.

The crackling stopped. It was human, the sound of that arrested movement. But Paul wouldn't be this sly. A twig snapped like a pistol shot, and the hair on the back of my neck began to rise. I held my breath and waited, but nothing stirred in the flat and brooding silence. A dark, human shape was crouched low, barely discernible in the layered shadows of the bushes.

The RV was at least half a mile away—too far for Paul to hear my call for help, too far to run. I dropped my sock and groped in the dark for a stick or a rock I could throw. My ragged breath was loud in the vacuum of sound as I picked up a dead branch.

"I've got a gun." My voice quavered. "Come on out."

The bushes stirred, making a whisper of leaves.

I lunged into the thicket, swatted the underbrush and connected with something solid. A jolt of satisfaction traveled through my bones until I heard the squeal of an animal and a long, panicked hiss.

Immediately my eyes and nose began to burn, and I was enveloped in the blistering, unmistakably pungent odor of skunk. My clothes were wet with the spray. A scream erupted from my mouth as I blundered through the thorny growth in my bare feet, threw off my shirt, unbuttoned my jeans, yanked them down along with my underpants, and stumbled out of them as I ran. Gasping, inhaling short bursts of air in a futile attempt to take in oxygen without taking in the smell of skunk, I bolted blindly through the woods.

By the time I reached the campsite the odor

was still sharp as a razor, caustic in my nostrils. I streaked past Paul, who was setting food out on the picnic table. He looked shocked at my nudity until he smelled me, and then he burst out laughing.

I flung open the door of the Winnebago and hurled myself into the shower, turned on the taps, poured a whole bottle of shampoo over my head and scrubbed desperately at my face and body. My feet were torn and bloodied, my legs were scratched and I was still quivering with shock as I stood under the weak spray from the nozzle.

Through the thin door of the bathroom I could hear him tromp inside, laughing. I burned with fury to think he found this amusing. When the hot water ran out I stepped from the shower, wrapped myself in my robe and sat on the toilet until I stopped shaking. I did not want to go out and face him.

But there was nothing else I could do, and eventually I stalked out, stiff with injured dignity. Paul was slicing tomatoes at the counter; he looked contrite, but the corner of his mouth was twitching. I walked past him, sat on the couch and picked up a magazine.

"Are you all right, Zoe?" he asked.

"No," I said coldly, turning a page. "I reek."

Paul laid the knife next to the cutting board and wiped his hands on his pants. "You're getting blood all over the rug—your feet are bleeding. Stay there, I'll get you some bandages."

It did not improve my mood to know that I should be grateful to him. Paul filled a basin with warm water and poured in a shot of hydrogen peroxide from his shaving kit, while I hid my face behind the magazine. The stench that continued to emanate from my body made it hard to breathe.

"What am I going to do?" I groaned. "It won't wash off!"

"I've heard that tomato juice helps kill the smell," Paul said. His voice sounded nasal because he was breathing through his mouth. He picked up my foot and dabbed at the pine pitch in the open cuts.

"I think that's an old wives' tale," I said. "Has this ever happened to you?"

"No," he said, smothering a grin. "How did it happen to you? You must have been standing right next to it."

"Christ," I said, shaking my head. "I hit the damn thing."

Paul bubbled over with laughter and tried unsuccessfully to stuff it back. "You hit it? Why would you hit a skunk?"

"Ah," he said, his lips moving against m neck. "You do like it."

"It's not a question of liking it."

"Haven't you thought about this?" he whis pered between kisses. "I have. I think about i all the time."

"I don't think very well when you do this, I admitted.

Still holding my arms stretched wide, h pulled my robe open by catching the fabric i his teeth and lifting it aside. My breasts wer exposed, and suddenly I wanted him to see me to touch me.

"You're beautiful, Zoe."

"You're too good at kissing," I whispered "Paul, we have to stop."

But his body listened to my body, and m body was on fire.

His hands released my wrists, and I left ther outstretched and limp when he lifted himself u to look at me. My eyelids felt heavy and m arms relaxed, while the globes of my bare breasts rose and fell with each breath. As h bent over me the hard muscle in his arms lightl touched both sides of my face as our lip brushed and parted.

The wind picked up outside and a pine con hit the roof, loud as a knock at the door.

›pened my eyes. I never should have let this ıappen. Paul wasn't thinking clearly, he'd regret t later, and this awkward memory would lie ›etween us every time we looked at each other.

I smelled awful. My mind was a snarl of unvanted thoughts, and I wanted to hide until I :ould find the cool, collected self I used to be ınd put it back on.

Turning my face away from Paul, I pushed ıgainst his chest and struggled to get up. He sat ›ack and watched me squirm out from under ıim, a puzzled expression on his face.

"What's the matter?"

"This is a mistake." My voice was hard. "I lon't want this to happen again."

I stood up and wrapped my robe tightly ıround my waist. Paul smoothed his hair. I natched fresh clothes from the closet and reeated again behind the closed door of the bathoom, the only place I could go to find privacy, he only place I could go to pull myself back ogether.

Six

The smell of skunk remained, a smell my nose would not get used to, a smell my mind could not ignore. Soon the Winnebago carried the odor in the upholstery. Even after two washings, the clothes I'd worn that night had to be thrown away, and they were my favorites—a bleached denim shirt and the most comfortable jeans I've ever owned.

Paul was driving on the morning we entered Montana. Every time I got up and moved around he watched me in the rearview mirror.

"Did I tell you we'll need a boat?" he asked.

"Why?"

"I buried the money on an island."

"An island in Montana?"

"In the river. The Missouri."

"You buried the money on an island in the Missouri River?" I repeated dumbly.

He nodded. "After I took the package from the guy I opened it, which I was not supposed to do, and then I realized what my dad was planning. I drove for about fourteen hours straight and finally stopped in Montana, near Fort Benton. I rented a skiff and found an island about fifty miles downriver. It's a big river. It's a big island, with trees and hills. I stashed the money there."

"So we're going to need a boat," I said, as if I were a character in a novel being written by somebody else.

"That's right."

I turned this over in my mind and thought, fifty miles down a river? In a skiff? With no guide but Paul? What was I doing? But I was more or less stuck; I'd just forced him to give back all his money, he'd agreed to let me decide if he should give back the rest, and I couldn't walk out on him and leave him stranded.

"How long a boat trip is it?" I asked.

"Four, five hours, tops," he said.

"Why can't we drive closer to this island? Fifty miles is a long way over water."

"It's all private ranch land or wilderness preserve. No roads. We could hike, but we'd have to trespass, it would take longer, and then we'd still need a boat to get to the island."

"Where can we get a boat?"

"Same place I did. Virgelle Canoe Company."

"They have motorboats, not just canoes?"

"I rented one there."

"Okay," I said, after a moment's hesitation. Part of me was appalled at the word coming out of my mouth, part of me expected a giant hand to descend from heaven and stop us both, but the me that was talking had already staged a mutiny, and she was ready to get on the roller coaster again, just for the fun of it.

The landscape of northeastern Montana was wide and green, acre after acre and mile after mile of green grass unrolling before us on hills that rose and fell in gentle curves to the horizon. Lark buntings perched in dense black rows on the barbed wire fences, scattering in all directions as the Winnebago went by. A storm was visible as it gathered on the horizon, fifty miles away. The wind whirled in advance of the rain to follow, pressing the tall grass down in wide swatches. Hawks and eagles soared on invisible corridors of updrafts and windshears, searching for prey in the open grassland.

As we drove closer to Virgelle I became more and more nervous. I wasn't sure Paul had the skill to guide us fifty miles down a river, and I knew nothing about motorboats.

"I'll drive," I said.

"Sure. Whatever," Paul replied equably. He'd been unbearably polite all morning. He braked to a halt and let me switch places with him.

After thirty minutes of bumping along country roads while Paul navigated, I pulled into Virgelle, a tiny settlement of farms on the northwest bank of the Missouri, thirty miles downriver from Fort Benton. The river looked high, brown as chocolate with spring runoff, moving smoothly but swiftly to the northeast. That was a good sign. The high water would even out the rapids.

I turned onto the dirt road approaching the Virgelle Canoe Company, a converted farmhouse that was also a bed and breakfast, according to the sign on the front porch. Once we were parked we stepped out of the RV and headed for the front door.

Antique tools covered the walls and the floor was packed tightly with old furniture, including several dressers with large mirrors. I looked in one mirror and had to smile. I'd washed my hair so many times in the last two days that it was full of static. Straight blonde hairs lifted off my head into a floating halo that swayed in the breeze created by the ceiling fan.

Another dresser mirror revealed the angled

reflection of Paul leaning on a counter of a marble-topped soda fountain. My eyes traveled slowly down the length of his body, a luxury I never allowed myself in the tight confines of the RV. His hip was cocked as he leaned against the counter and my eyes traced the curve of his back pockets under the yoke of his jeans. The girl behind the counter was eyeing Paul too, flashing a smile when he nodded to her. She couldn't have been more than eighteen. She was pretty. It irritated me to look at her.

I walked to the oak counter where a young man with a beard was counting ones into the drawer. "Do you rent boats?" I asked him after he'd counted the pile.

"Sure do," he said. "Canoes, paddles, life jackets, tents, all the gear you need if you're going downriver."

"No, I need a skiff, something with a motor."

"Sorry, ma'am, the one skiff we have is being worked on. Had to ship the motor on over to Great Falls about two weeks ago."

"You only have one motorboat?"

"Like the sign says, we're a canoe company."

"Will the skiff be ready tomorrow?"

He consulted a schedule hanging on the wall by the register. "Looks like it's gonna be at least another week. By that time you could probably canoe the whole river. Ever used a canoe?'

"Yes," I said, and weighed the thought of canoeing fifty miles. I knew about canoes. My father had drummed the skill into me all those summers ago on the Housatonic, and I knew I could still J-stroke in my sleep. Canoeing would mean camping out for at least one night. And ticks and rattlesnakes and storms. And sunrise, sunset. Wild beaches. A river.

The clerk smiled at me and reached out to shake my hand. "My name's John, I'm the owner here. How far you planning to go?"

"Fifty miles or so. Is there a place downriver where you can pick us up and shuttle the canoes back here?"

"You bet. The takeout is a bridge at McNulty Bottoms. It's about seventy miles. You can probably do it in two days with the current this high, but most people like to take a week."

I turned to see Paul sipping a mug of root beer, caught his eye, and tilted my head to indicate that he should join the discussion.

"What's up?" he said after he'd crossed the room.

"The skiff is out of commission. I'm thinking we could canoe the river, if you're willing to paddle."

"Cool," he said. He looked surprised. "You're up for this?"

I shrugged. "Why not? It beats waiting in the parking lot for a week while the skiff gets repaired."

John reached under the counter and brought out two river maps. "You'll need these." He unfolded one and pointed to the bridge at McNulty Bottoms. "This is the takeout. Whatever day you get off the river, you just give us a call from the gas station right before the bridge and we'll come and get you within two, three hours. We don't like to rush the river runners. You want to take a few extra days, camp out, relax, you don't have to worry about us waiting on you."

"I guess we'll be getting out there," I said to Paul.

Paul studied the map of the river, found an island, and tapped it significantly. "That's the one," he said. "Grand Island."

I turned back to John. "Do you run the shuttle?"

"If you give us a hundred dollar deposit."

"Looks like I'm going to give you a lot more than that," I said. "We need everything. Have you heard any news about the weather?"

"The channel nine weatherman said there's a

storm coming our way, but he always says that. Half the time it's true, and those are good enough odds for him."

"Do you sell rain gear?"

John shook his head. "You have any with you?"

Paul and I looked at each other. "Probably not enough," I said.

"You better get on over to Fort Benton, then, see what you can locate," he advised. "Things could get interesting on the river."

It rained in the night, a blustery squall out of the northwest that shook the Winnebago and rocked us with a sporadic heaving. I struggled to swim out of my dream, lurched awake, and realized I'd been shouting in my sleep. It was the same nightmare I'd been having for ten years, where I was locked in a closet and a man was on the other side of the door, waiting to kill me.

Paul stirred, sat up on the couch, and looked at me while thunder rolled in the distance, a delicate cascade of sound. He slid out of his sleeping bag and padded silently across to the loft, then lifted himself smoothly into my bed.

"It's okay," he whispered. "You're dreaming."

In the intermittent flashes of lightning I saw his face clearly, in quick bright pangs that flooded him with blue light and then left us in blackness.

I was warm with sleep and in spite of whatever had made me shout, my body was relaxed, limp, unguarded. The rain drummed against the roof. He was wearing briefs and nothing else, his skin like silk against my body. He burrowed under the covers, encircled my waist with his arms, and pulled me to himself greedily, firmly, without hesitating; his teeth nipped the skin of my neck and held it lightly, exerting a gentle pressure that made my heart flutter. I tried to remember why holding Paul was a bad thing, why I should resist. My hands lay passive, uncommitted, crossed over my heart.

Paul held my chin and bent down to kiss my lips while I drifted into the sensation of his mouth as it moved on my own. His breath was sweet. The tip of his tongue slid into my mouth and traced the tip of my tongue. Everything he did felt like a dream, a harmless state of suspended pleasure, disconnected from my good intentions, disconnected from consequences.

He pressed his erection into my side and lifted my nightshirt, and his face disappeared as he dipped his head under the cloth. I felt his hand stroking and lifting my breast to his mouth. My brief anxiety dissipated, a casualty of the weird logic that comes with greed. I wanted this. There was no question about it.

It was a luxury, a huge relief, to abandon myself to the intimate pressure of Paul's touch. His mouth enveloped my nipple as he squeezed my breast, and I held myself motionless to feel the slopes of my body as he trailed his hand across them. Dipping into the cleft between my legs, he pulled my thighs apart. I was wet. He touched the wetness, ran his finger along the petaled folds of my vulva, and plunged a finger into the heated, milky center.

Why not? Why not? Why not? My mind kept repeating the question and automatically rejected any reason to stop this amazing pleasure. I turned to Paul and slid my hands over the smooth muscles of his body, cradled the contours of his back, his broad shoulders and hard arms. Paul's hand crept through the slick, wet curls and I shuddered against the movement as his fingers spiraled against me, rubbing, coaxing. His breath was hot on my neck.

My body rippled with sharply ascending urgency and filled with ruthless, single-minded purpose as it lifted into an explosive and utterly silent climax. He held me tightly as I vibrated with aftershocks. Tremors sparkled down the length of my spine and sent waves of heat through my legs, and I collapsed into the bedding, limp, appeased, drunk with release. I felt completely satisfied, as if I'd never have to do this again.

The rain freshened, driving hard against the side of the Winnebago, noisy as a tossed bucket of nails. I released my grip on Paul's arm and gave him a little push. He slid out of my bed and stumbled back to his bed on the couch. After he fell back against his sheets I could hear him stroking himself, and when he came he grunted. A few minutes later his snoring started up again.

I lay awake, unable to sleep, stunned by what had happened. Now that it was over, why did I feel so pissed off? It embarrassed me, how fast my body had responded to him, how starved I must have seemed, how easy it was for him to masturbate me to an orgasm. No one had ever done that to me. Was giving me a hand job his way of showing off? Teasing me? Asserting some kind of dominance? The whole thing was weird, and now I felt like I owed him something.

The ground was muddy the next morning, and

by the time we packed the canoe with our gear and eighteen gallons of fresh water, we were streaked with brown clay. Our food was all neatly stowed in coolers and river bags John had given us, enough to feed an army for a week. I did not want to be hungry out there.

I'd had to visit the cash machine twice in Fort Benton to pay for all the supplies I kept remembering to buy. Paul offered to pay for some of it but since I was the one who'd impoverished him, I didn't want to cost him any more money. He didn't have much left. Once I wrote the check for the rental of the canoe and all the camping gear, my vacation funds were nearly gone, and pretty soon I'd be living on the money from the sale of the house. Not a good financial plan.

I rinsed the mud off my legs, then slathered suntan lotion on my face and arms. I offered the sunscreen to Paul, who shook his head and took off his shirt. "I'm going to catch some rays," he said, squinting up at the clear sky. His eyes were inscrutable behind the mirrored sunglasses. There was nothing in his voice to suggest we'd been rolling around in my bed the night before. It was probably better this way, with no change in our roles, no rocking the boat. My practical side had already taken over, like daylight rushing back into the body after a dream.

I threw my bag against the thwart of the canoe.

"I'm ready to stow my day pack and canteen," I said to Paul, who was clipping the bow line to the seat. "I'll paddle stern."

"Sure," Paul said, "I'll take the front."

"The bow," I corrected him. It annoyed me to see Paul grin as I said it.

"I knew that."

We waded into the Missouri up to our knees, the water so cold I flinched as it divided and splashed around my legs. My calves disappeared in the murk of the river, the muddy bottom sucked at my feet and I shifted my weight to keep from sinking.

The canoe was floating free. I stepped in. Paul clambered in after me and we settled ourselves amid the bags, canteens, boxes, packs, and spare paddles. The eddy caught us and propelled us toward the deeper current in the center of the river, and I steered us toward the riffles that signaled the fastest stretch of water. We were launched.

The neatly fenced pastures and outbuildings of Virgelle glided past us as we shot downriver toward the sculpted bluffs of the Missouri

Breaks. Soon the river was bordered on both sides by towering formations of white cliffs and lava dikes, the horizontal sedimentary layers folded and uplifted by ancient volcanic activity.

Paul pointed to a golden eagle circling above us.

"I keep reaching behind me for a seat belt," I confessed to him.

He laughed. "That is so . . . you."

I sat arrow-straight in the stern, holding my elbow fully extended as I imitated the J-stroke my father had taught me. Paul was facing the front, and there was no one to see me if I made a mistake. But I held my body stiffly, as if someone could.

Paul's stroke was vigorous but erratic, his rhythm thrown off by fish jumping or swallows skimming or any talking. He seemed to have no vanity about how he looked as he shoveled the paddle into the water, and I felt a twinge of irritation at his lack of self-consciousness.

My gaze was caught by the river disappearing under the canoe as the water drew us downstream with smooth, rushing ease. Whether I paddled well or poorly, whether I deserved the ride or not, I was being carried.

Why am I always trying so hard? I asked myself. Why do I have this white-knuckled grip on life? I loosened my clasp on the paddle and let my shoulders slump a little. Without even being aware of it, I'd been holding the cheeks of my buttocks tightly together. I separated my thighs, relaxed the muscles in my rump, and rested against the cane seat. The sky was a rich and bottomless blue. The eagle was still there.

"Zoe?" Paul said, turning around. "We're going in circles."

After a few hours of paddling, the sharp borders and straight lines of the road were long gone, and my thoughts began to wander. Time melted and curved into the hazy distance, sometimes folding in on itself so a memory could surface, clear and sharp as the sun on the water.

I remembered swimming with Marta in the pool at the country club. It was a stunningly hot day in June and the sky was white with heat. It must have been a hundred degrees in the shade. I wanted to stand in the pool all day until my skin puckered like a raisin. Marta was only four years old but could stay underwater for a long time, sitting on the bottom with her legs folded like a Buddha. I hated to put my head underwater because the water went up my nose and in my ears and it felt like drowning, but I held my nose and ducked under to check on my sister.

Marta waved, her eyes open and pink from chlorine. Little bubbles came out of her mouth.

I was thirteen years old, all legs and shyness. Already I knew how to shrink up against walls and turn silent as paint. It was safer to be invisible in our house.

Marta was a chubby little kid, loud and in love with the sound of her own voice, given to grand announcements and shameless exaggerations. She loved diving. When she tired of sitting on the bottom she swam out of the pool to bounce on the diving board.

"Look at me!" she shouted. "I'm a Lammatic Bomb!"

"Atomic bomb."

"That's what I said!" Marta ran back and forth on the board, her fat feet churning until she chose a spot to hurl herself into the water.

"Did I get you wet?" she asked hopefully when she surfaced.

"Oh, yeah," I nodded soberly, standing in water up to my neck. "I'm soaked."

When we walked home Marta wore her towel like a cape, safety-pinned around her neck.

"I'm Superman," she told me. "You're not."

"Hurry up, Superman," I said. "We're late."

When we were two blocks from home Marta's feet started to drag. It was time for her nap. She clutched my legs and slid down into a heap on the sidewalk and lay there with her eyelids fluttering until I picked her up. Her body felt boneless and limp, heavy as only a sleeping child can be. I carried her the last two blocks, and as I struggled to walk under the weight I pretended that Marta was my baby. I had always pretended that Marta was my baby, and this pretend mothering comforted both of us.

When we opened the front door I could hear my mother's voice in the downstairs study. Father Connor visited every Sunday to give Amelia communion and receive her weekly stipend to the church. It had been four years since she had left the house.

Amelia had sent us off that morning with the vague assumption that we were going to mass, and as always, she'd given me five dollars for the collection plate. The five dollar bill was folded at the bottom of my bag, under the wet towel. In my bedroom I took it out, smoothed it flat, and put it on the small, soft pile of these bills that I kept in an envelope under the mattress. Someday I would take all the money and go out west with Marta. We would be waitresses. We would live in a little apartment over a gas station and go camping on weekends.

We never went to mass anymore. Marta and

I left the house on Sunday mornings looking beatific, like child-angels, wearing dresses with lace-edged bibs and patent leather shoes, our bathing suits and a towel stuffed in my large straw bag. Amelia never seemed to notice when we came home late, sunburnt and damp around the collar.

I was sure my mother would never find out where we'd been. Amelia was becoming more and more isolated from the neighbors, the town, the outside world. She lived in her room, apart from all of us, distant as a saint, without friends and without any visible desire to procure them. The groceries were all delivered. Amelia bought whatever she wanted from catalogs. The maid shopped for my clothes until I turned thirteen, and then I bought them for myself with money my father gave me. As the days trickled by, my mother became more and more cloaked in a world of silent contemplation that no one could penetrate.

That Sunday evening Amelia set a place for Richard as she always did, although it had been at least a week since he'd shown up for dinner. In the past few months he'd disappeared into the city, attending parties and dinners and meetings that seemed to require his constant presence. When he came home he was usually in one stage or another of alcoholic stupefaction, either manic or morose.

Amelia used her grandmother's silver and monogrammed napkins and lit the ivory tapered candles as she did every night. The draperies were closed. The dining room was stuffy and dark, thick with the smell of food. Through a crack in the curtains, I could see the bright summer evening held at bay.

Amelia and Marta and I were all seated, about to say grace, when the front door creaked open. There was a brief silence, a moment's hesitation before the door scraped shut and we heard our father's footsteps on the carpet. Richard appeared at the doorway, steadying himself against the wall, smiling at the candles as he took his seat at the head of the table and nodded to us. His face was brightly oiled by gin, but he was still lucid, suspended in the glow of alcoholic bonhomie.

"Beautiful," he slurred, "beautiful girls."

I held my breath and counted out the exhalation. Lately I'd started counting to myself whenever we all sat in the same room together. I ticked off the moments from one to a hundred, then started again at one. If he raised his voice, my hearing sometimes disappeared.

But that night he was cheerful and relatively

coherent. We eased into our familiar roles. He piled his plate with rolls and creamed corn, slices of honeyed ham, and applesauce. His deep laugh echoed off the yellow rose wallpaper and vibrated the chandelier. He complimented Amelia on the dinner and drank several glasses of wine, but ate nothing.

"Such a soft life you little girls have," he said, twinkling at us. "So cozy. So sweet." He shut one eye and gazed into the claret colored shadows of his wine. "Sooo . . . expensive.

"I read something today," he said, his head wobbling slightly on his neck as he turned to look at me. His eyes glazed over. There was a longish pause.

"I'm listening," I assured him.

Richard closed his eyes and cleared his throat. "It was by Paul Gauguin. He wrote it when he was dying of syphilis in Tahiti. He said 'I shut my eyes in order to see.' "

"See what?"

Richard waved the fingers of his left hand. "Perfection. An ideal world. Paradise."

"I'd rather keep my eyes open," I said.

"Blindness is an acquired taste, I suppose," he replied. "Wouldn't you say so, Amelia? You've put the blinders on, haven't you? What is it you see?"

I was grateful we had so much food, because we were both ravenous.

That second night we were lazy and sore from the unaccustomed exercise. I had a touch of poison ivy on the back of my legs and a chronic ache between my shoulder blades, and these distractions dominated my sensual attention in an oddly pleasant, immediate sort of way. I watched Paul from a chaste distance. His body was turning brown, his long hair whitened to platinum by the sun.

As the canoe slipped downstream the next morning, my eyes drifted across the water and the heaps of debris from last year's flood. The view changed minute by minute, in a seamless passage of islands and cliffs. A great blue heron squawked and flew before us, its long neck folded into an S, the slow beat of its wings making me wonder how such an unlikely looking thing could defy gravity.

The river was several hundred yards wide, a flat expanse of water that flowed around and in between large islands. Some of the larger islands were thick with groves of cottonwoods and meadows of big bluestem and buffalo grass. Wild primroses were just coming into bloom.

Paul's bare back flexed in the sunlight as he feathered his paddle. After the first day he'd settled into a quick and powerful rhythm that left me with little to do but steer while he provided the horsepower. When I dug my paddle in the water to match his pace, we knifed through the water with surprising speed, forming a wake that curled and splashed away from the bow.

On the third day we reached Grand Island and camped early on the south bank. The island was probably two miles long, with a grove of cottonwoods along the high bluff in the center of the island. The beach where we landed was overgrown with rose bushes that pricked my legs when we dragged the canoe ashore.

Paul seemed nervous and bustled back and forth with boxes and bags until the boat was empty. When I saw he was setting up his tent, which was something he usually put off until the last moment, I confronted him.

"Why don't we go dig up the money?"

He finished tapping a tent stake and wouldn't meet my eyes. "I don't know how to tell you this."

"Tell me what?" I prepared myself for bad news.

"There is no money."

"What?"

"There is no money."

"What?"

"I told you, there—"

"I heard you, don't tell me that again."

"But it's true."

"Oh, sure. You just want to keep it."

"Zoe. There. Is. No. Money."

"I saw the money with my own eyes, Paul. You said you stole it. Where's the rest?"

"I lied, okay? I didn't take any bribe money."

"Then where did the hundred thousand come from?"

"I stole it from my dad."

"Why?"

"He tried to cheat me out of it. My mom left it to me for my twenty-fifth birthday, but he told me he wouldn't give it to me until I got a job."

"So you stole it."

"Not right away. I got a job with one of his clients, managing a hardware store, but I got fired. I hated it. Wearing a tie every day is just not my thing, and besides, my boss was a jerk. He used to hit on one of the girls who worked there, fondle her butt in front of the other guys who worked there. She hated him but she was only eighteen and afraid to lose her job, so I called him on it and he fired me. My dad didn't believe my side of things. He said I didn't deserve my mother's money, he was going to keep it and teach me a lesson."

"So then you stole it? Or is this just another lie? Let's see, I'm having a hard time keeping track, Paul; first it was the lottery, then a bribe from unscrupulous developers, now it's just because your daddy was mean to you?"

"My dad keeps a vault in his office. I've always known the combination—he wrote it on the underside of his desk blotter when he had the safe installed. It's my mother's birthday. Not something I'd forget. So I figured, he thinks I'm an asshole anyway, why not take what's mine?"

"But why'd you send the hundred thousand back to him, if it was yours?"

"I didn't."

"But I saw you mail it."

"You saw me mail him a bag of socks. I dumped the money in my sleeping bag when you went up front to get me a pen out of the glove compartment, and then I jammed some of my socks in the paper bag."

"So you sent your father a couple of dirty socks, registered, certified, with a note saying 'Will send the rest soon'?" I would have laughed if I hadn't felt so bitter.

Paul shrugged.

"Why did you tell me that story about the other hundred thousand? Why bring me out here?"

"I wanted to disappear. Give him a little time to cool off."

"And you used me to do it."

Paul looked at me. "Yeah. I did. Are you sorry?"

"Why did you have to lie? Why didn't you tell me the truth?"

"Because you never would have come here. You would have dumped me."

"What if I had? You could have found a way to disappear by yourself."

He grinned at me. "You had that cute little RV and nothing better to do. That last night I was at my dad's I saw an article in *Field & Stream* magazine about this river. There was an ad for the canoe company in it, and I thought it looked like fun. I saw that picture you keep in your address book, the one of you and your dad canoeing, and I knew you'd go with me if I gave you enough reasons to get on a river. Come on, admit it. It's been fun, hasn't it?"

He didn't know I'd been lied to by Jake for the past four years. Paul had no idea how much he'd made me hate myself. I would never learn this simple truth: Men lie. The lies Paul had told me, lies I'd swallowed with hardly a moment's doubt, were choking me. Was everything a lie? Did I look like the kind of person who would believe anything? Was this some flaw I could control through cynicism, or did all men just naturally want to lie to me?

"So you got everything you wanted and you didn't even have to pay for it," I said.

"I'll pay you back, if you want to make such a big deal out of it."

I held my hands up, palms out. "Just stop talking, okay? The more you talk the more I want you to drop dead."

Adrenaline shot through me and I walked off and kept on going until I'd reached the other side of the island, out of his sight. I sat on a rock and stared across the dirty water. This vacation was over. I'd had it. I didn't believe his latest story any more than the others. He was a liar and a thief and I was probably lucky he hadn't conned me for more than the price of a few meals, some gas, and a trip down the river.

"You're a fool, Zoe," I said out loud. "Cut your losses and get out now." These thoughts were even more bitter because they were so familiar. When would I ever learn anything? The next few days would be hell, but at least I hadn't slept with him, not in a real way, not in a way that counted. I squirmed thinking about how he must have been laughing at me behind my back. Making up one whopper after another and then pulling those halfhearted attempts at seduction. I wanted to kill him. I wanted him to disappear, all right. I wanted him to jump in the river and drown.

It was the fact that he'd used me that made me feel the worst. I'd paid for everything, leaped at the chance to rescue him, drove him to Montana, and then I gave him a canoe trip. He must have thought I was the stupidest, most gullible woman he'd ever met.

Why had I done it? What magic did he possess to erase all my hard-won cynicism and convince me to do these things? He was young. I'd assumed youth meant innocence. But there was more to it than that, and it galled me to admit it, but he was right. I had that cute little RV and nothing better to do. My life was so empty and miserable and unbearable I couldn't even stay in San Francisco to visit my sister. Everything Paul had proposed doing was something I'd wanted to do, and somehow he knew that, he knew just how to lead me along by offering me exactly what I really wanted, even when I didn't know what I wanted. I'd even wanted the sex.

For now it seemed best to ignore our last conversation, get through the rest of the night and tomorrow and get off the river and leave him for good. I walked back to the campsite determined to show no emotion, just efficiency.

Paul was standing by the tent, shoulders slumped, head bowed. He turned as he heard me approach.

"I'm sorry, Zoe," he said.

"Forget it," I said.

"I have to tell you something, but I'm afraid you'll be mad at me."

Too late for that, I thought, but held my tongue. "Go ahead."

Paul bit his lip, turned his head, and looked off over the sun-dappled water. "My mother died." His voice was so soft I could barely hear him. There was a long pause.

"I know," I said.

"Last December," he said.

"You told me she died when you were a baby." Another lie, I thought. I was keeping count, now.

"She died last year. Cancer. At first there were three little shadows on the X ray they were worried about, then there were five, and then they popped up everywhere. She was gone in six weeks."

He looked at me then, to make sure I was listening. "She left me all her financial assets. Mutual funds, stocks, bonds, T-bills. My dad was her executor. He wanted me to leave everything up to him, the way she did. Keep the money invested."

"And you didn't," I said.

"No. I forced him to sell everything, cash it all in. It made him furious. He told me I'd made nothing but shitty decisions in my life, told me what a disappointment I was. I was supposed to be like him, a breadwinner, steady, ambitious, a number-cruncher. He's always been Mr. Dependable, with an office full of plaques for Employee of the Year. I'm not like that."

"No," I agreed dryly.

Paul shot a glance at me and went on. "He was crazy about my mother. Every Sunday he went to the bakery and bought her a cake with writing on it. 'Bon voyage' or 'Happy Birthday,' even when it wasn't her birthday or she wasn't going anywhere. She loved him. They could turn the lights down low in the living room and slow dance to Perry Como on a Wednesday night. She was so—" his voice broke, and he swallowed noisily. "—gentle."

He ran his hand over his face and continued. "She was the buffer between my dad and me. My mom was outgoing, friendly, adventurous, curious. Like me. But he squashed that side of her. He was afraid of it, afraid it would hurt her, get her into trouble he couldn't fix. He was always afraid of something bad happening to her.

"I used to tell her about working on ships, the storms, the fights, the strange cities—Yokohama, Liverpool, Bremerhaven. Her eyes lit up. She loved it. I was like her lighter self. I was the one who escaped him."

"So why risk losing the money she left you? Why didn't you put it in a bank?"

Paul shook his head. "It never scared me, to have her cash with me, to risk losing it, the way I did the day I met you, when you took off with my duffel bag. It was okay to risk it. The money felt sweet to me, like her, as though she'd finally distilled herself into something I could carry with me wherever I went, a chunk of currency, something meant to move back and forth, to be exchanged for comfort and freedom and good times. I wanted to keep that money with me because I wanted to feel her, the way she loved me. I needed her. The money was her last gift to me. I wanted to keep it close."

I was speechless. Paul sat down on a dead cottonwood log and stared at the ground near my feet. "I'm sorry I lied to you," he said, stiffly, formally. "It was easier to lie, but I know that's no excuse. I just didn't think I could explain it. I didn't think you'd believe me."

I hardened my voice, made it cool and businesslike. "I'm not sure what I believe anymore," I said. "Let's just get through this and get off the river. I don't think I can go on traveling with you after all this."

"I understand," he said. And we didn't speak again for an hour.

The weather had been clear and fine, the air warm until midafternoon, but now the wind picked up and the temperature dropped rapidly. There were heavy clouds moving in from the southeast. I watched them intently, studying the wind and the thickening cloud cover.

The clouds gave me something else to worry about. Maybe I had no radar for the wrong men, but I knew weather, and those clouds meant trouble.

"You think we'll get more rain?" Paul called to me when he saw me staring at the sky.

I walked over to him, took off my hat, and ran my hand through my hair. "We need to get off this island."

"Why?"

"I don't like those clouds. They look yellow to me."

Paul tilted his face back to study them. There was a greenish tinge to the dark undersides that bellied low toward the ground.

"What do you think?" he asked.

"I hate to say it, but those are tornado clouds."

"Christ, Zoe! Are you sure?"

"See how they swell out underneath? It may be nothing, they may swing west of us, but it sure looks like it's going to hit somewhere close by. That means it'll probably rain like hell even if it misses us. Let's get out of here while we have the chance. We need to find a more secure campsite, above the flood plain."

We re-packed the canoes in silence. I numbed myself to the reappearance of the old, familiar ache in my chest by performing the mindless tasks of stowing gear and tying down the load. The paddle in my hand was a dead thing. The canoe was a dead thing, an insensible object to be used and discarded. There was no magic in any of it anymore. I was way out in the middle of nowhere with a liar, and the only thing I wanted to do was get through the bad weather ahead and get rid of him.

We paddled in silence for another three-quarters of a mile until we came to a beach that led to high ground sheltered by a cliff to the south.

If the storm continued on its present course the cliff might spare us from the brunt of the wind. The clouds boiled along the horizon and a green light flickered across them. I didn't like the looks of what was headed our way.

When we disembarked I faced Paul and issued orders.

"We need to drag the canoe all the way out of the water so we can tie it down. When you set up your tent, make sure the rain fly is battened down well. Put the rocks on top of the stakes, the heaviest rocks you can find. Forget dinner. We need to leave the kitchen packed and covered and weighted with rocks. It's going to blow like hell in a few hours."

"I'm right behind you," Paul said.

Seven

The outfitter had given us an old garbage can lid for campfires, along with the admonition that ashes and charred wood had to be buried before we left a site. Paul built a fire on the beach, and we warmed our hands over it while the night turned cold as winter. I shivered in my jacket.

"It's going to be a long day tomorrow if the weather doesn't break," I said, chunking another piece of kindling on the flames. "Feels like snow."

"In May?" Paul asked.

"Spring is tricky in the West. I've seen it snow in Santa Fe every month of the year."

"We made good time today, though," he said. "We must have come twenty-five miles."

In the distance there was a dull, hollow roar, a dim rushing sound unlike anything I'd ever heard before. "Do you hear that?"

"What is it?" Paul asked in a whisper.

"Wind?"

"Wind or water," he said, cocking his head. "I don't like it."

We stared into the fire and listened intently as the roar grew closer. An eerie high pitched whistling emerged from the night like the howl of a freight train bearing down upon us.

The wind struck. A shower of sparks exploded from the fire and disintegrated in an instant as the cinders were swept a hundred yards up the beach. We watched in shocked dismay, unable to move until we heard a loud knocking and banging, a sound like baseball bats being cracked together.

"The canoe!" Paul yelled.

Stumbling in the dark, we ran to the grassy verge where it had been tethered. The canoe was gone.

"Paul!" I shouted, pointing up. "Look!"

The dark silhouette of the canoe was revolving in an invisible whirlwind, rope tethers flying loose, stakes banging against the sides. The huge black shape rose in slow motion and hovered before us as I held my breath, electrified, paralyzed.

The canoe flew into the darkness and disappeared. A few seconds stretched into a long, timeless moment of uncertainty. The wind whipped our clothing and cold rain began to drive against our faces. The canoe will crash down on our heads, I thought, but I stood frozen, caught, unable to second guess the whirlwind.

There was a tremendous splash out in the middle of the river. I could see the dim outline of the canoe, flipped over and twirling in the water, quickly slipping downstream. Paul ripped off his jacket, sprinted toward the sound, and plunged into the freezing black water.

"No! Let it go!" I shouted, running after him.

I could barely see Paul's head bobbing in the dark water, his body swept downstream until he vanished in the blackness, swallowed by an avalanche of rain and wind that formed whitecaps on the river.

"God damn it!" I cried in exasperated fury and fear. "God damn it to fucking hell!" I raced along the beach until my breathing was hoarse and panicked, but there was no sign of Paul.

The cliff stopped me. It loomed ahead, slick with rain, a dark and vertical barricade that dropped straight down to the water. I would have to backtrack at least half a mile in order to scale it, and by then Paul could be washed up anywhere. The rain had turned to icy sleet and was driving against me in gusting blasts that threatened to knock me flat. My hair was soaked, my jacket as wet as if I'd been swimming in it.

I staggered toward the water while the wind clawed at my clothes and nearly blew me over.

"Paul!" I screamed into the freezing rain. The wind was unlike anything I'd ever seen, a brutal, continuing force that felt like a hurricane. Thirty feet away from me a cottonwood began to lean toward the river, making a loud sucking sound as its roots pulled out of the earth. The huge tree broke and cracked like gunfire as it thundered down into the water. Sticks and branches and leaves flew horizontally through the air, and sand struck my face like buckshot.

Lightning danced across the water and sleet hammered my face. He'll be all right, I muttered to myself. He'll get to shore. I'll find him.

I looked longingly across the water, into the darkness. Uprooted trees raced by on the waves, the dark silhouettes of their branches making treacherous sweepers that could easily snag Paul or knock him out.

A branch flew hard against my back and shoved me headlong into the shallows. The icy water stung my skin, stripped the warmth from my body, and sent a cold, liquid shock traveling through my bones. I jerked myself back toward shore, heaving against the current. The river was choked with drifting logs and felled trees that could charge against my body—or Paul's—like battering rams. In the bright and constant cracks of lightning, the river looked malevolent, lit by the cold electric fire in the sky. My fingers were numb, my bones frozen.

Get warm, I told myself. Get dry. The storm had become a fury unlike anything I had ever witnessed, a clamor of wind and thunder that forced me to bury my head in my arms to smother the noise. The wind-driven downpour slapped against my body, and then the rain turned to hail that drifted in white windrows along the shore and bobbed in the water.

I dragged myself, stumbling, toward the place the tents had been. I was tilted into the wind, half-blinded by the slashing hail. Halfway there my leg caught on an exposed cottonwood root and I fell to the ground. I was dazed and slimy with mud.

"I can't do this by myself," I screamed at the sky. "You have to help me!"

There was no help coming from that sky or its macabre light. I heaved myself up and stood for a moment, panting to catch my breath. Shivering had turned into spasms. I staggered on and rested every twenty feet to catch my breath, face bent down to shield myself from the airborne debris that lashed me like bullets. Pellets of frozen rain collected on the inside of my collar, then trickled down my back.

My tent was blown over, but still holding to the earth. I rigged the center pole upright and held it there while I wriggled inside and kicked the sleeping bag into the corner so it wouldn't get wet from my soaked clothing. In the dark I fumbled for a flashlight and flicked it on. I was shivering and my hands looked blue. My teeth rattled. I pulled roughly at my clothing and tore off my jacket and shirt while my fingers throbbed, clumsy with cold when I pushed at the hard edge of the buttons. I stripped down to the skin and threw my wet clothes outside, then squeezed my body into the sleeping bag. My skin was cold as marble, and my body shook convulsively.

I hugged my body tightly, helpless with urgency, angrier than I'd ever been in my life. We were in trouble, big trouble. I was hypothermic. I knew about hypothermia. My neighbor's son had died of hypothermia. Only eight years old, out on his first camp out, he wandered away from his family right before it started to rain. They found him the next day, just two miles from the campsite. This had happened in July, a thousand miles south of here, in the hills outside Santa Fe.

Paul was somewhere out there in the hail, without shelter, without dry clothes, in temperatures that had plummeted below freezing, not to mention the wind chill. Could he survive this night? He had almost no body fat to insulate him. I tried not to think about the ribs that were visible under his skin, or the broken trees in the river, or the long night before us.

My body was piercingly, shockingly cold, shuddering and numb everywhere, except my nipples and toes and fingers, which throbbed with pain.

I continued to grip myself tightly, my teeth clenched against the damp and frigid chill. The tent luffed in the harsh wind, and only my body kept it from blowing away.

After an hour or two I quieted. My skin was slightly warmer. The thunder had receded and the rain had settled into a monotonous drumming. The tent was leaking in one corner but the sleeping bag was dry. I slumped in exhaustion and fell into a troubled doze that swirled with bad dreams.

In the dim first light I woke, opened my eyes, and sat up. The twilight was only beginning to lift the darkness into day, but it was time to get started. In three minutes I was dressed, my pockets stuffed with granola bars. I squirmed out of the tent and stepped out into the dawn. The wind was still as I picked my way over the ground to Paul's tent, which was plastered against the trunk of a cottonwood. I shook out Paul's duffel bag from the dripping nylon folds, grabbed his binoculars, and set off toward the canyon to the north.

I needed to find a way up the ridge overlooking the river. The ground was slick and muddy. In the litter of cottonwood branches that had broken in the wind, I could see the path the tornado had taken through our campsite. Several large trees had been uprooted and lay on their sides in a crush of tattered green.

The sun rose in a clear sky, and I gnawed on a granola bar as I walked. Tumbled boulders in the mouth of the ravine blocked my way and I struggled over them. A pair of bald eagles flushed from their roost on a dead juniper and cast long shadows on the ground, but I plunged ahead without stopping to look.

My lungs were burning by the time I gained the top of the ridge. I drove myself on, half trotting along the grassy summit. I reached a lookout point that afforded me a view of our campsite, as well as a string of islands downriver where Paul might have found shelter.

I settled the binoculars against my face and scanned the river. On the second island to the east, just past the cliff, I saw a glimpse of white, the color of the canoe, under a clump of brush at the western tip of the island. There was no sign of Paul.

I would have to go back to the camp and float down the river with the paddles. Get the canoe and then scout the river for him. I flinched at the thought of swimming in the icy river. There was no other way to reach the island. It's not that far, I muttered under my breath, trying to reassure myself. And I have no choice.

On the way down I leapt from boulder to boulder, covering ground with a speed that would have terrified me a month ago. Back at the camp I stripped off my dry clothes and put on the wet ones from the night before. I grabbed a life preserver, then tucked both paddles under my arms and walked into the freezing current.

The sight of the dark, muddy river filled my eyes like an enemy, and I waded into it with a determination that kept me from hesitating as the water rose above my knees. I gave myself to the current, let the water pierce my skin and sweep me toward the narrows by the cliff. The rapids bobbed me up and down like a cork. An icy wave washed over my head, and I panicked for a moment as I submerged, then kicked my way to the surface and gasped for air. My foot knocked against a rock, but my flesh was so chilled I couldn't feel the bruise.

The canoe came into sight as I rounded the bend in the river, its white flank gleaming in the sun on the beach. Reaching with my toes for the graveled bottom, I kicked against the current and slogged my way through the shallows, then struggled out of the water and flailed my way to shore with a paddle in each hand. My toes were so cold it hurt to walk.

When I lifted the canoe I saw Paul's inert body underneath it, sprawled lifelessly on the wet sand. He's dead, I thought dully. You wished him dead, and now he's dead. He always gave you everything you wanted.

I had never seen a dead body before. It held a grayish pallor, a terrible chalky, ashen color. It looked empty, slack, like a mannequin: The mouth was frozen open, sand coated the lips and the side of his face. Nothing alive could be so still.

I didn't want to touch his corpse, I didn't even want to look at it, but I turned him over carefully and bent my head low to listen to his chest. Nothing.

Maybe his heartbeat was too low to hear. I tore off Paul's wet clothes and undressed myself in the cool morning air, dropped to my knees and lay beside the body. I tugged him close until my belly was pressed against his back, my legs crooked slightly to warm his legs, my arms wrapped tightly around him. His body was stiff and cold, hopelessly cold, and my mind wheeled away from the grisly pietà we formed. I closed my eyes to everything, to the dead boy in my arms, to the stony beach, to the sun beating down on our nakedness.

I kept my eyes shut and wondered in a detached, idle way how long I should wait before I gave up. A canyon wren trilled in the distance; mournful, descending notes sounded three times before I let myself move. Paul was dead. My eyes filled with tears and I let them fall down my face unchecked, the spidery rivulets running into my mouth. Paul's shoulder was like a stone as I leaned my head against his body and let the sobs plow through me, through him, out.

And then anger flooded me. I was furious at Paul for dying, and fury was a relief, it gave me something to feel besides this raw pain and loss, and I clung to it because soon I would have to get up, and it would help if I were furious. All these things passed through me at the same time my eye was caught by something odd, something out of place, something impossible.

Paul's shoulder was covered in goose bumps.

My mind twisted back on itself and gave me a spurt of energy, like an unexpected desire to laugh. A door opened in the hard wall of evidence, and now the downy blonde hairs on Paul's neck were standing on end.

The bumps pricked his skin all the way down his back and around his waist, and I watched in disbelief as one patch after another rose in shivering life.

"You're alive," I said in a small voice. I took my first deep breath of the morning, and it felt like a balloon filling me up, lifting me.

"You're alive," I said again in a louder voice that cracked with relief. Rubbing Paul's skin roughly, urgently, I pressed myself to his back and moved my hands up and down his arms while the sun bore down on us with increasing strength as it flew up in the clear sky.

The day continued fair but Paul remained in a shivering, unconscious stupor. Our clothes dried on the sand. It was getting warm.

I had to pack up the camp and bring it to Paul. He needed to drink hot liquids, and both of us needed food. But I had no idea whether I could get past the cliff, paddling upstream by myself.

I unwrapped my arms from Paul's waist to get the canoe ready. It felt good to stand up, shake out the cramped muscles in my legs. I dragged the canoe down to the grassy shallows. When I came back I covered Paul with his dry shirt and wrapped his pants around his legs, then pulled on my clothes.

At the water's edge I walked the canoe out a few feet from shore and took the stern seat, then shoved off with the paddle. The eddy next to the island provided a strong reverse push that jettisoned the canoe thirty yards upriver, but soon the channel narrowed and I was forced into the rapids by the cliff on one side, boulders on the other. The rapids made a dirty, pounding foam against the rock face. I angled the canoe as close to the boulders as I dared and paddled furiously against the charging current.

It took almost ten minutes to gain another thirty yards. The nose of the canoe trembled as I fought to keep it pointed upstream. If I let the pressure off for an instant I'd be sucked into the rapids and smashed against the granite face of the cliff. Over and over I dug my paddle into the water, gouging, plowing against the current to push the canoe through the narrows.

Finally the bow jerked free and the canoe slid out on the broad, slow part of the river. My arms burned with effort as I aimed the canoe to slice diagonally across the current and traverse to the other side.

Once I reached the campsite and jumped out, it took less than five minutes to throw all our equipment in the canoe. Nothing was folded or stowed and I squashed the tents on top of everything, the fabric held down with frying pans, bags of oatmeal, hiking boots, and the Coleman stove.

The trip back to the island was swift, with the current working for me. Paul was in the same position, still unconscious, and I wrapped him in sleeping bags and built a fire on the beach to warm him, using stove fuel on the damp wood.

Finally Paul groaned, turned his head to the side, and vomited up brown river water. I wiped his mouth and covered the bile with sand.

I made him a cup of soup but it spilled down his chin when I tried to pour it into his mouth. His eyelids fluttered but didn't open. I tucked the sleeping bag tightly around his neck and placed my hand on his cold, damp forehead. My throat ached when I looked at him.

Edging down beside him, I held his muffled body tight in my arms. Something inside me came to rest when I held Paul, and even though the circumstances were horrible, the quiet of my body as it held him was welcome. With my cheek against the plump, swaddled curve of his shoulder, I was unafraid. His neck smelled good. The sun was warm. I waited for Paul to wake up and look at me.

The snap of twigs in the fire brought me out of a light doze. The fire was hot and my armpits were damp. Paul wasn't shivering anymore. His eyelids were still, his breathing steady, and his color was good. The spasms of shivering had come and gone all day, but now his skin was warm to the touch. I reached for the mug of broth and brought it to his lips. He swallowed, then coughed while I whispered encouragement.

His eyes opened.

"Hey there, stranger," I said. "I was worried about you."

Paul gave me a feeble smile. "Hey," he whispered.

"Don't talk if you're too weak."

"I'm okay. I have a headache, that's all."

"I'll get you some aspirin," I straightened myself and rose to my feet as if an invisible weight had slid from my shoulders.

"Get three," Paul said.

When I came back he knocked them back and looked at me. "Are you all right?"

"I'm okay now. You scared me to death."

"Believe me, I scared myself."

"I thought you were dead." I brushed a strand of hair off his forehead.

"You weren't the only one." Paul's voice trembled.

"Can you sit up and drink some soup?" I asked.

Paul struggled to sit up and held out his hand. "Give it to me. I can sip it." His voice sounded hoarse.

I passed him the mug but let my arm remain on his back, cradling him.

"How did you find me?" Paul asked.

"I ran up that ridge this morning and looked downriver." I gestured with my chin toward the cliff.

"How far down did I go?"

"Just a half mile or so. Around the bend. Not far."

"It felt like I was swept along for miles."

"What happened to you last night?"

"God, it was noisy," he said, closing his eyes. "I never thought a storm could be that loud. It didn't take long for me to grab the canoe but it seemed like forever before I got to land. There was all kinds of trash bumping up against me. The water was ripping."

He took a drink from the mug and continued in a gravelly voice. "All I thought about at the time was how far we'd have to walk out with no canoe. Forty, fifty miles? I just couldn't stand to see it disappear."

"You're lucky you got to the island."

"I pulled the canoe over my head for shelter. The hail was a bitch. I must have bruises all over me. The ground was soaked, I was soaked. At first I couldn't get warm and then it was weird, but I got sleepy and I didn't feel cold at all. I passed out, I guess."

"Next time, Paul? Let the damn canoe go."

"Hey, I learned my lesson. I feel like I've been hit by a truck. I feel like shit."

The sight of him sitting up, alive, gave me a rush of gratitude so intense I reached out and put my hand to his face. "Don't ever scare me like that again," I said in a wobbly voice.

He put his hand over mine, cupped my fingers with his fingers, and leaned into my palm. His cheek was warm. I listened to the wood crack in the fire, felt the connection of our hands and the wind ruffling my hair. Something was taking shape inside me, a kind of courage, a willingness to be foolish, and it was slowly forming out of the knowledge that I had been lonely for a long time.

"I don't want to lose you," I said.

Eight

The days grew hot, bringing mosquitoes in the evening. I was alert to the slightest change in the wind or weather, but the heat comforted me. We stayed on the island where I'd found Paul for another two days to give him time to recuperate.

We spent hours lying on the beach the next day, baking ourselves in the sun. Paul had a deck of playing cards in his shaving kit, and he taught me a game called "What the Hell." I hated the game, which went on for hours.

"Your bid," Paul prodded me, a stem of grass dangling from his mouth. His eyes were masked by mirrored sunglasses, his face shaded by a baseball cap.

"What's trump again?" I asked. The sun on my belly made my sleepy.

"Hearts," he said, rearranging his cards.

"Oh, three, I guess," I said. "Although I've lost all hope of ever getting my bid in this lifetime." It irked me that I couldn't predict how Paul might foil my plans, turn against me without warning, and steal my tricks or dump unwanted ones on me.

"Hmm," Paul said, leading with trumps, the ace of hearts.

I yawned. "I'm quitting. It's too hot. I need to rinse off."

"You can't stop now," Paul said. "This is my best hand yet."

"Gee, you make it so hard to leave."

"Don't get sarcastic with me, young lady. I'm an invalid. You should be pampering me."

I looked at the deeply tanned and comfortably sprawled body in front of me. "I think you've made a brilliant recovery. You look healthy to me. Why don't you go make dinner?"

"No respect!" Paul cried. "The tornado veteran gets no respect whatsoever!"

I pulled myself up slowly and brushed the sand off my clothes. The heat made me slow and sultry, aware of the weight of my breasts in my bathing suit and the muscles in my legs that were softened by the warmth of the afternoon. I had tied my T-shirt in a knot high on my belly. Now I undid the knot and pulled the shirt off over my head.

The top of my bathing suit was gritty with sand and scratched my skin. I peeled down my shorts, careful to keep them from scraping my sunburned thighs. My back was turned to Paul but I knew he was watching.

"If you want to skinny-dip, go ahead," he drawled. When I turned around his eyes were invisible behind the mirrored glasses, his mouth relaxed and serious.

The idea was tempting. It seemed stupid to worry about being naked in front of him after yesterday's drama. I'd held him for a long time without a stitch on either one of us, just to press warmth back into his flesh. Even though he'd been unconscious at the time, it seemed as though our bodies already knew each other.

I undid the hook in the back and let my bathing suit top fall forward. The sloping flesh of my breasts prickled in the breeze, and my nipples shrank and hardened as I felt Paul's eyes on me. With slow, deliberate movements I peeled down the lycra bottoms and stepped out of them. I was damned if I would hurry out of a sudden attack of shyness, although it was embarrassing to stand before him, revealed in all my thirty-nine-year-old skin.

All my life I had looked at myself in mirrors, making judgments according to the reflection. Now the only view I had of myself was this foreshortened caricature. When I looked down my breasts looked like pale, rose-tipped triangles. My belly curved out like the side of a melon, and only a few dark wisps of pubic hair were visible below it. My thighs narrowed down to the nearly invisible points of my knees.

Moving self-consciously, knowing I had Paul's undivided attention, I picked up the two pieces of my bathing suit, folded them, and put them down on the sand beside Paul's seat.

"Don't say a word," I said sternly. Paul nodded. He put his fingers to his lips and made a motion of zipping them shut. I turned and walked back to the river, the sand hot under my feet. The water was heart-stoppingly cold, but I waded through the shallows and dove in, hooting at the shock.

By the time we broke camp and moved on, the heat wave was upon us. It must have touched ninety by midday, and I slipped out of my clothes to skinny-dip again when we stopped for a break after an hour of canoeing. It seemed stupid to put them back on. When Paul saw that I wasn't going to cover myself back up he took off his pants and threw them up in the air. The pleasure of not wearing clothes overwhelmed my shyness, and after an hour I didn't even bother to hide the softness of my belly when I bent over to tie my shoes. With no mirrors around I forgot how to pose. When we made camp I was still naked except for my shoes, and my limbs swung freely as I walked, wrists loose, knees springy and flexible. I stood with my belly curved out and my shoulders relaxed.

Paul didn't put on pants until it got dark, and in spite of the bruises on his back, his body looked comfortable, natural, unguarded. To my eye we looked real in a way that clothed people didn't. From then on Paul and I paddled naked on warm days, until the sun grew too strong and we shielded our heads and legs with whatever was close at hand—a towel, a T-shirt, a baseball cap. The river had gone down and the current was more sluggish, so we'd paddle in the morning for five or six miles and then stop for the day. Paul was a little slower, calmer. I wasn't sure how much of a beating he'd taken on the inside from hypothermia, but his outside looked just fine.

On the fifth day after the storm I sat on the bank of the river and leaned against a chunk of driftwood. The late afternoon sun glistened off the sweat between my breasts. For the past week we hadn't seen another soul on the river, and the stillness was deep. A column of mayflies swarmed above the shallows and a trout dimpled the surface of the eddy, sending concentric rings rippling in larger and larger circles.

In the clearing behind me Paul hummed in a low voice, but the tune was muted by wind and distance. I could see the peach colored flash of his skin through the trees, and the glimpse of his body soothed me.

Creating a river cuisine brought out an ingenuity in Paul I'd never seen before, and I loved the way he cooked for me. He'd badgered me into buying a cast-iron pot with a heavy lid for the trip, and I considered it my best investment. By removing the top and venting the bottom of an empty juice can, he created a tight, efficient column for burning charcoal briquettes. Once they were white hot he'd scatter the glowing coals over the lid of the pot, then seat it on hot coals underneath. The heat was surprisingly even and provided us with an oven, and an oven meant cornbread, carrot cake, pie, and biscuits, all the starch we craved from living outdoors.

His menus were varied and delectable. Baked chicken and yams, freshly caught trout and baked potatoes, linguine with pesto, riverside spaghetti. Paul used cabbage, carrots, raisins, figs, dried pears, plums and apricots, nuts, jicama, green and red bell peppers to mix up fresh salads every night. He made it look easy, and I was grateful for the strange gift of being in the wilderness with a man who created one gourmet meal after another, while I lay on the bank of the river and let my muscles turn to molasses.

The air had a shine to it. The buttery light clothed the many shades of green, while cottonwoods rustled in the heat. A leaf fell toward me, kissed the surface of the water, twirled like a green paper boat and drifted downstream. It had been at least an hour since I'd had a thought in my head, and all I wanted to do was to go on not thinking until dinnertime, go on listening to the river beating like a giant watery heart against the rocks.

That was how I felt when Paul was out of sight. But when he was around, I began to feel restless. I monitored the distance between us, and I was aware when it changed by a fraction of an inch. I was aware of his hand brushing mine when he passed me a canteen or a playing card. His hand never lingered. He watched me but he didn't make a move toward me, and for the first time, I wanted him to. Something about his new indifference bothered me. For weeks I had been locked into a stance of automatically resisting his overtures, and now there weren't any overtures to resist. He was cheerful and easy around me, but didn't touch me, didn't make sexy jokes, didn't even bump up against me accidentally. It felt odd, as if I were suddenly invisible, or sexless. I didn't like the feeling.

That evening I sat on the bank of the river watching a kingfisher preen on a dead branch that hung low over the water. Paul lounged nearby, his fingers laced behind his head, his body lit by the setting sun. The low light caught the edge of his face and made it glow, giving him a slender, bright halo. A strand of his hair lifted in the breeze and the sun turned it into a thread of fire. My heart beat high and fast in my chest when I looked at him.

"Hey, Z," Paul spoke easily. "What's up with you? You've hardly said two words all day."

I slapped a mosquito. "I was wondering about those stories you told me. The lottery. The developers. How did you come up with all that?"

"It's just the way I am. I'm good at making up stuff and saying whatever comes into my head."

"Why do you lie?"

"Most people want to hear something besides the truth, don't you think? Like, whenever they ask, 'How are you?' "

"You think I wanted to be lied to?"

"Sure. You wouldn't be here if I'd told you the truth."

"Do you know how to tell the truth?" I jumped up and pulled my shirt on over my head and stuck my feet back in their flip-flops. "Or are you going to spend the rest of your life running away from it?"

"Are you talking about me or you?" he asked.

"What do you mean?"

Paul took the grass stem out of his mouth and pointed it at me. "I'll tell you some truth. You are in one bitchy mood. What's eating you? Do you want to talk about it or are you going to run away?"

I sat back down, crossed my arms, and glared at him. "Seems like that's exactly what you're always doing. Running from consequences. Punishment."

"Maybe I am," Paul said. "Not many people like to get punished."

"Then why do you want to hang around me?" My voice cracked.

The corner of his lip twitched. "For the sex, what else?"

"That's not funny."

"Zoe. I like you, okay? There's got to be some kind of bullshit detector in you that knew that all along."

I thought about Jake and his mistress. Where was my bullshit detector then? But it was true. I had known. And I hadn't wanted him to tell me the truth about it. For the last few years I'd spent most of my energy plastering over the cracks in our marriage, smoothing our conversations, never confronting Jake when we went for months without making love. I'd wanted to preserve the lie that we were happily married.

"It's too easy to excuse yourself by saying people want to be lied to," I said. "How would you like it if I started lying to you?"

Paul laughed. "I don't think you can. One look at your face and I can usually tell what you're thinking."

Uncertainty stabbed me. If that were true, then he knew I'd spent the last two days thinking about lifting his hand and kissing the inside of his wrist. And other things.

"Well, it's a nice evening," Paul said lazily, his bare chest rising and falling with a yawn. "I guess I'll take a walk." He started to stand up.

"Wait!" I said, more sharply than I intended.

"Why?" Paul asked me, frozen in midair. "What's the matter?"

"There's something I need to ask you," I said, and blushed to the roots of my hair. What now? Just spit it out?

"Go ahead."

"Oh, Christ, Paul," I sighed. "I'm so bad at this."

"Bad at what? What do you mean?"

"Nothing," I muttered, and walked away before I made myself look like an even bigger fool.

In my tent I threw myself down on my sleeping bag and buried my face. Where was my competence when I needed it? What did it matter if I could install a jacuzzi but couldn't seduce a twenty-eight year old kid who had already been salivating after me for more than three weeks?

In my mind I tried to shrink Paul to a liar, a thief, a stupid boy, a nobody. It didn't work. I wanted him. My body hummed with desire whenever I looked at him and saw the ripple of muscle in his back, or that sly smile and the slice of his dimple. The sound of his voice pulled me into a state of longing that could only be cured by fucking or absence, and in this case, absence was impossible.

Each moment was sharp when I was with

him. The hiss of the Coleman stove in the morning, the splash of hawks hunting fish in the river, the soft sucking sound of the canoe scraping against a muddy bank all gave me a visceral thrill of pleasure because he was there, hearing it, seeing it, feeling it with me. I was poised on the edge of reaching for him no matter how dazzle brained it seemed. I was sliding into a kind of strenuous hunger that made me more reckless every day, but I didn't care. I wanted him.

On the sixth day we traversed a broad curve of sluggish water between Deadman Rapids and Iron City Islands. I steered the canoe straight across the curve and almost ran us aground as we passed over a tongue of submerged beach. The sandy bottom was less than a foot below us as we slid over the drowned yellow grass.

"I had no idea it would be this shallow here," I apologized to Paul.

"You couldn't know," he said.

"I should have. The current is usually faster on the outside of each curve, where it digs a deeper channel."

"What about rivers that are straight? Does the current go down the middle?"

"All rivers meander," I said.

"All rivers meander," Paul echoed. "I like that."

The borders of the river changed from day to day, the line of beach shrinking or expanding according to sun, rain, or wind. All its edges wandered. The meandering river, the changing sky, and the sloping irregularities of the landscape were free of right angles, squared-off ceilings, or doors. There was a constant flow of weather above us and river below us, an endless, seamless changing that included me, that carried me.

Under the sky all day, I spent hour after hour watching the swirl of water created as my paddle carved the current. The tail of the canoe wagged against the thrust of my stroke and curl, the repeated J that I wrote in the water, over and over.

The smell of our sweat mingled with sunscreen and a scent of woodsmoke. My attention wandered along the primroses that bloomed in ragged clumps along the bank, to the avocets that stood in the shallows and stabbed at minnows with their thin, curved beaks. I felt strong, like an animal, and the canoe was a part of that animal self, a slender white wing that carried me north, then east, then south, winding across the body of the earth. The sky was blue as a baby's eyes, the clouds white as milk, the river a rippling, meandering highway. I wanted this to last forever.

I kept a hat on all day and my sunglasses made a dent on the bridge of my nose. When I took them off I could still feel my river hat and river glasses, like ghosts on my face, heavy in the imprints they left behind.

At lunch I noticed Paul staring at me, his eyes assessing, weighing something hidden. I could feel myself respond with a tingling attention in my body, a warm restlessness in my thighs and belly, a readiness that broke into my reverie. My whole body wanted him. I felt like an animal in heat, a sow, a dog, a snake. But an animal would know what to do. An animal wouldn't be cursed with this shyness.

I woke in the night to the harsh squalling of raccoons. Every night they fought over the contents of the cooler. We couldn't afford to lose any food, and the noise was horrible. Why didn't Paul wake up and get rid of them? It was his turn. Muttering to myself, I tossed my sleeping bag aside and put on flip flops before unzipping the tent. I ducked out, picked up a stick, and charged them, hissing, whacking the ground until they fled.

After refastening the bungee cords and tucking a thermal blanket over the cooler, I paused to sniff the breeze. It was a balmy night. The air was warm, a thin cloud cover veiling the stars. I stood and stretched, fists in the small of my back, chest thrust forward, face lifted to the waxing moon. When I started walking back to the tent I saw Paul sitting on a dead log by the beach, facing me, the light from the moon catching his long loose hair and turning it white.

I walked toward him, swinging my hips, feeling potbellied and sensual, slow from sleep.

"What are you doing?" I asked when I reached the log.

"Watching you do battle."

"Why didn't you stop them?"

"I thought you might get up," he said with a lazy smile, "and then I wouldn't have to."

"You stinker," I said sleepily, rubbing my eyes with my knuckles.

"Have a seat."

My palms began to tingle. Instead of sitting, I walked behind him to stand at his back.

Slowly, delicately, I gathered his long hair in my hands and combed it with my fingers. He bent his head in pleasure as my fingers grazed his scalp. I could see goose bumps rising on his neck, visible even in moonlight.

"That feels great," he said. "I want you to do that for a million years."

His hair was thick and cool and I let it trail through my fingers. I was wide awake now, heart knocking. Holding a palmful of his hair off to one side, I bent down and blew lightly on the back of his neck. Paul shivered.

"Please tell me I'm not dreaming," he whispered.

"Do you want me to stop?"

"Don't even joke about it," he said, his voice tight.

Slowly, I lowered my face and kissed the nape of his neck. His soft brown skin was smooth against my lips, and when I licked the bumps of his spine I tasted salt. He held himself motionless, hardly breathing as I brushed his neck with my lips.

"I want you," I whispered against the whorl of his earlobe. I let go of his hair and ran my hand down along his arm, my fingers trembling. When I tugged his elbow he stood and faced me.

The watery moonlight gave our bodies a glow, a dreamlike softness, like foxfire in a meadow. Under the drawstring of his shorts his erection lifted the fabric. When I took him by the hand a spark went through me, a little shock and shiver of joy, and I led him downstream to a bed of matted grass and leaves.

Laughing softly in anticipation, I pushed Paul down into the grass with my palms flat against his chest, and when he fell he took me by the wrists and pulled me down on top of him. My flip-flops fell off. His chest felt smooth and tight with muscle as he wrapped his arms tightly around my waist, and when he kissed me I could feel the length of him, the solid flat of his belly, the long cords of muscle in his thighs, the slippery fabric of his shorts, and the hardness underneath. I took his face in my hands and kissed his mouth. His fingers moved over me, cupped my buttocks and squeezed them.

We paused to look at each other as I rose and knelt above him, smiling at the eagerness in his face. He was so familiar and yet completely strange, and it shook me that he could excite me so much. His eyes closed as I explored his face with my hand, and he turned to kiss my fingers as they brushed his lips. When he opened his mouth I let him lick my fingers one by one, and I stroked his tongue in a lazy back and forth motion, like a promise. When I knelt on the ground between his legs I could feel my vulva opening to the black night.

He cupped his hand around my breast and

lifted it to the warmth of his mouth while I shut my eyes and surrendered to the sensation of his tongue, the gentle pull of his mouth suckling me. I slid my fingers under the waistband of his shorts and tugged them down. His penis lay taut against his belly, the hard swollen pillar of it exactly fitting the curve of my palm.

Paul groaned, and it made me bold to hear his voice, so choked with desire. Gently, delicately, my fingers traced the hard ridge and the bow-shaped cleft at the top. A drop of clear liquid formed there, and I touched it with the tip of my tongue, tasting the salty, silky fluid. Paul thrust his hips toward my face but I knelt back, teasing him. My body was so aroused it felt as though it was no longer made of dense, hard flesh and bone, but becoming liquid, light, flowing like a river, opening out to a wide sea.

Paul's breath was ragged and uneven as I licked the tip again, and he cried out wordlessly as I took him all the way into my mouth. The thick shape was heavy on my tongue. My mouth cupped the weight, sucking. I could feel his hands gripping my shoulders, and when I lifted my mouth from him and looked up, his eyes were black in the moonlight.

"I want to touch you," he pleaded.

He pulled me up by the waist and I felt my

breasts pass over the slick wetness of his erection as I lifted my face to his mouth. When he gathered me in his arms, I kissed him lightly at first, then hard, pressing against the ladder of ribs that hid his heart, trapping his hard, wet penis against my belly. He twisted above me, tugging at my legs until they were stretched wide apart. I was open as a lily.

Leaning up on one elbow, he lazily drew his hand along my thighs, brushing against the wet curls of my pubic hair, pushing lightly with the back of his hand into the warm, slick center.

"Do you like that?" he asked softly.

"Yes," I gasped, lifting my hips to encourage him. My arms were limp on the grass.

With one finger, then two, he entered me, moving gently, slowly, in and out, lightly stroking and circling in a languid rhythm. When I shut my eyes, the delicate spiraling of his fingers made my whole body shiver with a strong rising pull, like a kite about to break its string.

My skin sang with tense, sustained delight as I lay in the tall grass and let him play with my body, his mouth grazing my nipples, then descending to my belly to lick the hidden crease in my navel, finally going further down to the damp warmth between my parted thighs. As he nestled in the fork of my legs, I groaned under the wet weight of his tongue as he licked me. Only an animal could be as shameless, as ready as I was. My breath came fast and I felt a hard, wolfish greed as the first long rolling breakers of orgasm gathered in my belly.

He slithered over me until his mouth was on my neck. I traced the taut swelling of his cock.

"I want this," I whispered.

"Take it."

I wriggled out from under him, pushed him down again into the long grass and knelt above him, my knees straddling his sides. His face was bright, alive, filled with joy.

I grasped him and lifted myself, hovered for a moment above his hips, then slowly settled down upon the shaft, drawing him into the center of my body.

Our joining smelled like the ocean. I rode him in soft, dreamy circles, taking him deep into me, pushing the tips of my breasts against his hands, my nipples hard as cherries in his palms. I heard the river rushing past us, the wind sighing through the cottonwoods, the shrill ringing of the crickets in the grass.

When I finally collapsed on top of Paul he twisted his body over to lower me back to the ground. His arms were taut and sweating as he lifted himself high above me and stabbed me again, penetrating the center. There was no gentleness in either of us after that. My thighs clasped him as he pumped violently into me. An avalanche of feeling burst loose inside me, cracking me apart with a force that was almost like pain.

"Oh God," Paul grunted, clutching me and holding me still. "If you move a muscle I'm going to come."

I held my face to his chest and heard the pounding of his heart. My body was slick with sweat.

"Go ahead," I said in a husky voice. "I'm ready."

"No," Paul said, "I want to do this all night."

"Then we will," I whispered, and covered his mouth with mine.

My body gripped his as we came together in waves that rippled from the center where we were joined, vibrating along arms and legs and extending beyond fingers and toes until I felt the dark night shatter into a sparkling blackness, laced with tiny explosions of color.

Paul opened one eye. "I'm still hard."

"I know," I said, smiling, my eyes open.

We remained locked together. His arms were warm and damp, his body pressed close to my own, and I could smell the rich intermingled odors of sex and sweat. Above his shoulder I saw the stars, the moon, and the drifting clouds. The moon's reflection wavered in the river like a lantern, until the wind broke the surface and scattered light everywhere.

Nine

I woke up the next morning alone in my tent, the sun already high and beating down on the orange nylon. Paul was cooking breakfast, and the smell of coffee drifted into the tent. My whole body was sore but I couldn't stop smiling. Stretching my hands up to the dome of bright fabric above me, I flicked the sun-dappled cloth with my fingertips. I loved this tent. I loved this river. By now the smell of willow and mud and water had filtered into my dreams, and when I pressed my nose into Paul's hair last night I could smell the river in him.

Long sleeves today. It was cool. I wriggled into warmer clothes, slipped my hand into the pocket of my sweat pants and found the compact mirror I'd brought and forgotten to use for the past week. I pulled it out, opened the scratched cover, and stared at my reflection.

The face that looked back was unfamiliar: The brown skin held a fan of delicate white lines around each eye where the sun hadn't penetrated the inner folds of my squint. My eyes were green as the moss by the river, bright and serene, the shadows from the accident gone from my face. I looked as though I'd recovered from a long illness.

I folded the glass image of the stranger back into my pocket and put on my sneakers. We were going to paddle today.

"Good morning!" I sang out as I emerged from the tent. "Isn't it a beautiful morning? Don't you just love the smell of coffee on a morning like this?"

"Hey," Paul said with a sly grin. "How'd you sleep?"

"Not much," I said sunnily, pouring myself a cup from the kettle.

"You're sure in a good mood." He beamed at me and leaned over to kiss my cheek. I smiled at the frying pan.

"These are almost ready," Paul said, wiping his hands on his shorts. He flipped the pancake over, picked off a burned part and ate it. "Hungry?"

"You bet." I put my coffee down, unzipped

the pack where we kept the plates, pulled one out, and opened the cooler for the syrup.

There was no food left. No margarine, no syrup, no more pancake mix. We'd come to the end of our trip. The bridge where the shuttle was meeting us was only five miles away, an easy paddle that would only take an hour or two.

"This is our last day," I said.

Paul gave me a crestfallen look. "We can't keep on going?"

"We'd starve."

"I could snare us a duck."

"Yeah, if you could talk it to death. 'Just follow me, Mrs. Duck, and we'll go dig up a million dollars. I've got the map right here.' "

Paul laughed. "Or you could boss it to death."

My mouth was full of dry pancake, but I had to object. "I am not bossy."

"You are so. You're the queen of all bosses."

"Okay, you're right. I am bossy. You do the dishes."

"Yes ma'am," Paul said, and snagged the last piece of my pancake with his fork.

A dirty green van came for us at McNulty Bottoms, just below the bridge. The driver waved at us as we pulled the canoe from the river. Cars and trucks roared above us on the concrete span, and the noise broke over me like the sound of gunfire. The pillars sunk in the river, the highway gouged through the hill, the beer cans glittering in the weeds: every sign of civilization hurt my eyes.

We unloaded the canoe rapidly. The boxes of food and jugs of water were empty and weighed almost nothing. Hoisting the canoe over our heads, we lifted it to the top of the van and cinched it in place with nylon straps.

We sat next to each other in the back seat of the van while we rattled over the dirt roads to Virgelle. I leaned against Paul. I was sore from our lovemaking. I was happy. It felt like I'd finally figured out how to make life get good, and now I would never have to go back to being lonely. Paul looked at me and tried to smother the smile that kept threatening to take over his face.

"You still look like a wild thing," he finally said, pinching my cheek.

"I loved it," I said, "feeling wild."

A moody wind sprang up and the gathering clouds produced a thin, wind-whipped rain that pelted the windshield in long, vertical slaps. I caught myself digging my heels against the floor of the van, as if to brake our quick progress back to Virgelle. I missed my old cane seat in the stern and the unbuckled sway of the canoe. The canoe had felt like a part of me, and it felt strange to know it was tied to the roof of the van like a discarded pair of wings.

The Winnebago was parked where we'd left it in the lot next to the canoe company. The day had turned bright again, and I unlocked the side door, stepped in and felt a wave of affection for the small interior and its tightly packed fittings. It felt like home.

"Looks like everything's okay," Paul said, crowding in behind me.

"You want to take a shower first?" I asked.

"You don't?"

"I'm going to call my sister."

"Okay. Meet me inside for lunch when you're ready."

Paul began to shed his clothes and I watched him, enjoying the strip.

"God, I stink," Paul said.

"I like it," I said. "It kind of turns me on."

He nosed his armpit and shuddered.

I laughed. "Go shower."

Paul tossed his dirty clothes into his duffel bag and sashayed into the bathroom with a clean towel draped over his shoulder.

I punched the numbers for Marta's apartment

in San Francisco. Her answering machine clicked on and I heard my sister's voice on the tape.

"Zoe, if this is you, call Mom. I'm at her house. I'll talk to you soon. Call Mom."

Perspiration beaded under my arms and trickled down my sides as I dialed the number in Connecticut and listened to it ring.

"Hello?" It was my mother's voice.

"Mom? Are you all right?"

"Oh Zoe, I'm so glad you called. I have some bad news, honey. Daddy is dead. Our Richard is dead."

My knees buckled. I couldn't believe what my mother was saying. I sat down on the porch step, one hand before my face. "How?" I whispered.

"He was weeding in the garden and he fell over. It was a massive heart attack. A myocardial infarction, the doctor said. He didn't suffer long."

I didn't trust myself to speak. I clutched the edge of the step.

"The funeral was yesterday," my mother said softly. "Marta knew you'd call and wanted us to wait, but we just couldn't keep waiting. He's been dead for a week now."

I bent over, unable to catch my breath. The sun stared down and the earth didn't move and

I put my hand to my heart to make it start beating again.

When Paul came out he took one look at me and stopped drying his hair. "Zoe? What happened?"

"My father is dead."

I felt a sharp rush of vertigo. The walls skidded and swirled when I turned to look at Paul, and everything in the room seemed to throb. Bracing myself against the door, I concentrated on his slurred face.

"He died a week ago."

Silence filled the cabin.

"Are you okay?" Paul finally asked.

"No," I said, sinking back, giving in to the dizziness. The report of my father's death seemed grotesque, impossible. My voice sounded as if it came from outside my body, each word stretched as if it were coming from the end of a long tunnel.

"Zoe, I'm so sorry." Paul's eyes were grave. Someday he'll know exactly what this is like, I thought. The notion that Paul would go through this kind of shock and pain made it real, and a thick film of tears blurred my vision.

"I have to go back there," I said in a ragged voice.

Paul took my hand. "I want to go with you."

"Okay," I whispered. It didn't matter. What might have panicked me yesterday was nothing now. If Paul wanted to come or stay, it was up to him—he'd have to take care of himself. I could barely sit up.

I leaned forward again, rocking the visible world with every movement of my eyes. "I have to get a flight out of here."

"I'll call the airlines," Paul said. "We can leave the Winnebago at the airport. Do you need anything else?"

What I needed was more than he could provide: a turning back of the clock to the hour before this one, when I was whole. I need my dad, I thought, and immediately felt engulfed by the fresh and awkward sorrow I'd been holding back. The spinning earth came to rest as I reached toward Paul to hide the tears that spilled down my cheeks. I wept into his shirt, sobbing against his neck like a child.

"I'm so sorry," he said, his expression tender with borrowed grief as he folded me into his arms.

Paul held my hand at the gate in Chicago where we had to wait for a connecting flight. I studied his hand as if it were a stranger's, as if I had never seen it before. Paul was alive, in a body that would eventually die. This seemed like the most important thing about him as we sat together in plastic chairs. I knew I was moving like a robot. There were too many people smiling.

"Can I get you anything?" Paul asked.

I shrugged and stared out the window to the empty tarmac. "No."

Paul jingled the change in his pocket. "I need gum for the flight—you sure you don't want anything?" I shook my head. "I'll be right back." He walked off to the newsstand down the corridor.

I hugged my purse and stared out the window, leaning my head on the cool glass. My mother was waiting for me. I wanted to comfort her, but how? I hardly knew her. She'd always been a shadow, a pale, polite woman who faded into the woodwork whenever my father was around. My father was such a strong presence that she flattened herself to make room for him. Maybe she'd be different, now that he was dead. I hoped so. I used to pray that he would die, when I was younger. I'd always thought of him as her jailer. Her fear of going outdoors had to be connected to his being the way he was.

No one in my family ever had the nerve to stand up to him. He drank too much. He was unfaithful to my mother. He ordered my sister and I around as if we were slaves. But I could not shake the sense that the center and source of our lives had vanished, and what remained might not be strong enough to hold together, or even remotely resemble a family.

When Paul returned he was wearing a brand-new shirt—a white, buttoned-down, short sleeved shirt with blue pinstripes. His pants were new too, I noticed—dark brown, with a leather belt I'd never seen before and a shiny pair of loafers.

"Do you think these are okay?" he asked. He looked self-conscious. "There was a men's store over on the B concourse, and I thought I should try to get something a little more appropriate."

"You look like a pillar of the community," I said. He looked different. It made me uneasy, how different he looked.

"I want to make a good impression," he said.

"It doesn't matter," I said. "You look just fine."

The plane banked low over the trees and leaned toward the pale expanse of the Atlantic. The Manhattan skyline poked through the smog and the air in the cabin became warm and humid, smelling like air that had been breathed already by millions of people.

Paul craned his head to look past me, eagerly scanning the view. He'd been holding my hand for hours and his grip was cutting off my circulation. Hoping he wouldn't notice, I delicately freed my fingers and massaged them in my lap.

Paul looked younger as we drew closer to Connecticut, and I felt a growing anxiety about introducing him to my mother and Marta. I was wearing one of my old suits, a charcoal gray number I used to wear when I had to go talk to my loan officer, with a silk shirt that came up high against my throat. Paul's new clothes made him look even younger, like a teenager trying to look like a grown-up. His ponytail needed brushing, and it didn't go with the ivy league clothes. Everything about him looked false.

Why was he here, anyway? When I looked at him I felt exasperated, nagged by his thoughtfulness. He was trying too hard. He'd been too quiet on the long flight, too solicitous and solemn—he didn't move around or act naturally. Only a sliver of time had passed since I'd rolled around with him on the grass by the river, but now I felt detached. Gradually the armored coolness of my upbringing tightened and hardened like a second skin around me. I was isolated inside this detachment but I was safe. It was just like coming home.

Four years had passed since I'd been in Connecticut, four years since I'd seen such high layered walls of green: Bright maples, huge oaks, and towering hickories billowed against the dark skirts of spruce. The light slanted through the trees and spilled across the wide lawns and sidewalks of Westport. When I rolled down the window in the cab, the air carried the scent of last night's rain, a rich mixed odor of water and earth. At the top of the sloping street I could see a flash of white clapboard and the red brickwork of clustered chimneys that crowned the roof of the house where I grew up.

I knew every house as the cab drove up the block: the Clarks, the Bullocks, the Taylors, the Shaws. In the fifties the neighborhood had been full of kids my age. Donny Shaw was a heart surgeon now at Johns Hopkins. Melinda Taylor was a housepainter, living in Vermont with her lover and their three-year-old son. Petey Clark had died last year of AIDS.

We used to play kick-the-can or hide-and-seek or sardines during the long summer evenings. I could still remember hiding in the latticed crawl space under the back porch, crouching by empty flower pots and split bags of peat moss. One summer evening we all lay in the middle of the street as if we'd been run over. The blistered tar had smelled like oil, black and warm against my cheek. We waited for a victim, and eventually a Cadillac had breezed up the road, its headlights sweeping over our inert forms. The car slowed, halted. An old man opened the door and hurried toward us. He stood over me and spoke in a shaky voice. "Are you all right?"

"We're dead!" I yelled up at his face. We jumped up and streaked off down the hill, laughing and whooping as the sound of his angry shouts grew faint in the gathering darkness.

"Is that your house?" Paul asked. The cab was turning up the long paved drive.

"Yes," I replied absently, fumbling in my purse for the fare.

"Wow."

"Could you get the bags?" I asked him, angry that he was so impressed with the house. It had always been like this, with every man I'd ever brought home. Their eyes glazed over and they all shrank into themselves at the sight of the old Georgian house on top of the hill. To me it just looked like home, my father's trophy, my mother's prison. The dazzling white pillars of the front portico rose to a sloping roof, with dormer windows on the third story accented by black shutters and a decorative fence around the rooftop. A New England garden in full bloom flanked both sides of the drive.

The garden was always gorgeous in the spring: the forsythia, the hyacinth and daffodils, then tulips and lilac, and now the rhododendrons and azaleas, bright as fire against the dark green lawn. I led Paul up the trellised walkway to the porte-cochere. Roses lined the path and wisteria blossoms hung from the arbor, dangling over our heads like fragrant bunches of fruit.

I knocked on the side door, then tried to open it. It was locked. There was a muted stirring in the house, and then the curtained glass door opened.

My mother's hair was white as chalk. I was so surprised at this that I didn't notice my mother had answered the door. Four years ago Amelia had refused to stand in the open doorway.

"Zoe!" my mother cried, flinging the door open wide. "And who is this?"

Marta appeared behind my mother and rushed over the threshold to grab me in a violent hug. "Get me out of here before I kill her," Marta whispered in my ear.

"Paul, this is my mother, Amelia, and my sister, Marta," I said in a strangled voice as Marta hung from my neck.

"So this is Paul," Marta said in a tone loaded with innuendo. She let go of me and swept her eyes over him. "Pleasure to meet you."

"Likewise," Paul said.

"Come in, come in," Amelia said breathlessly. "We'll all be more comfortable inside."

We sat on loveseats in front of a curved glass china cabinet in the living room. At least fifty floral arrangements were banked around the enormous fieldstone hearth, and the smell of rotting flowers was intense. I longed to open a window. The thick Persian carpets swallowed every sound. The damask curtains were drawn and the room was crowded with furniture and shadows.

"You look sunburned," Amelia said, smiling anxiously at me.

"You look different," Marta said. I looked at Marta and thought the same thing. Marta's hair was longer and unkempt, lying flat and unspiked on her head, straggling into her eyes. Her face was pale, her eyes raw from crying.

"Could I have a glass of water?" Paul asked.

"Of course, dear. Would you care for juice or a soft drink?" Amelia said, rising smoothly from her seat.

"Water would be fine," Paul said.

"Is he old enough to drink?" Marta asked, turning to me. "Maybe he'd like a beer."

I ignored her and looked at my mother, who paused in the doorway. "I'll take some juice," I said. Amelia looked shrunken, her white hair aging her by twenty years. Her face was still fine-boned and classic, pale as porcelain, but she seemed thin, fragile, and when she left the room there was no sound of her passing.

"So where have you been?" Marta asked, reaching into the silver candy dish on the coffee table. I scrutinized my sister's face. No eyeliner. No lipstick. She looked gray, like an underdeveloped photograph.

"Montana."

"Doing what?"

"Canoeing."

"You should have told me, Zoe. We were frantic because we couldn't reach you."

"How's Mom?"

"Same as ever. I'm ready to leave. Dad's Lincoln is still in the garage. I thought you might give me a lift to the airport."

"Jesus, Marta," I said. "We just got here."

"Oh, I'm well aware of that," Marta said. "I'm the one who's been stuck here for six days, nine hours, and forty-three minutes, all by myself with the nutcase."

"How was the funeral?"

"Mom had the whole thing done right here at home. The service, the mass, three or four hundred mourners and eighteen zillion floral arrangements. I thought she might bury him in the living room. Stick the body in the trash compactor and slide the remains under the rug."

"So she didn't go to the cemetery."

"Mom? Go out that door? Surely you jest."

"Did you go?"

"Of course I went. Along with hundreds of people I'd never laid eyes on. I was the only blood relative to watch the box go down the hole."

"I'm sorry, sweetie." I didn't like the tightly coiled look in her eye.

"Compared to the way he died, the funeral was nothing. Didn't she tell you?"

"What do you mean, the way he died? He had a heart attack."

Marta leapt off the sofa and crossed the room, her footsteps silent on the thick rugs.

"Mom was playing the piano when she saw him fall over. He was outside the window, right here." She yanked open the stiff draperies and light flooded the room. Paul and I instinctively put our hands up to shield our eyes from the glare.

"See this bush? There's a dandelion under it. See? It's still there, still growing. Dad went out to pull it up himself and when he bent down to get it he just kept on falling. He collapsed right in front of her."

All I could think was that my father must have hated the way he died, gasping under a peony bush, at the mercy of his housebound wife.

"Good old Mom! She called 911! It took them ten minutes to get here, then another twenty minutes to get to the hospital." Marta whirled around and faced me. "He might have lived, Zoe."

"Maybe," I said, my heart twisting.

"What if she'd been halfway normal? She could have given him CPR, she could have driven him to the hospital, she could have—"

The sound of a tray crashing to the carpet brought us all to our feet. We turned just in time to see Amelia cover her mouth with her hand and run from the room.

"God damn it!" I sputtered. "What do you think you can accomplish by blaming her,

Marta? He's already dead, isn't he? Are you trying to kill her too?"

"I want her to change!" Marta yelled back. "She is perfectly capable of going outside! We've all been covering for her for so long we just accept it!"

I knelt and placed the broken shards of glass on the tea tray, soaked up the puddle of water and juice with a napkin.

Marta stopped in front of me, yanked my arm, and lifted me up. Her face was filled with hatred, and I wanted to smother that look, stuff it all the way back to childhood, where it belonged.

"I remember running out the back door one day when I was six," Marta went on. "I was just outside in the yard, not twenty feet away from the door. It was a beautiful day. There was nothing wrong. Mom started shrieking at me from the window to come back in. I went back inside and she slapped me across the face, hard. 'Don't you ever run out like that again,' she said. I didn't know what I'd done wrong. She made me spend the rest of the day up in my room."

Marta let go of my arm and paced the room, not bothering to lower her voice. "She's had analysis, she's had therapy, she's had every fucking faith healer money can buy and the bottom line is, she won't go out because she doesn't want to. Well, I'm sick of it. When her little self-centered phobia starts killing off people I love, I'm going to get pissed."

I was speechless as I contemplated my sister.

"She's the reason Dad is dead," Marta whispered.

"But he is dead," I said. "Accusing her is not going to bring him back."

Marta aimed a kick at the heavy silver tray and sent it flying across the room. Glass shards and wet napkins bounced to the carpet as the tray soared through the air and shattered the front of the china cabinet with a spectacular clash of breakage.

Marta gave me a steady look of challenge. "I know accusing her doesn't bring him back, but it sure makes me feel better."

I searched the house until I found Paul lying on the bare mattress in the unused maid's room at the top of two flights of stairs. It was a tiny, Spartan cubicle, with a sloped ceiling and a single window overlooking the front lawn.

"So this is where you disappeared to."

"Did you find your mother?"

"She's locked herself in her bedroom. Marta

seems hell-bent on breaking every dish in the china cabinet." I had left Marta standing in broken glass, flipping Spode plates like frisbees into the fireplace.

"How are you doing?" Paul asked.

"I'm tired." I nudged him over and lay down by his side on the mattress.

Paul covered my hand with his own and with my nose just a few inches away I saw how soft the back of his hand was, the skin smoothly stretched and padded and sprinkled with downy blonde hairs. My own hand was bony, the tendons visible as they radiated from my wrist. The skin around my knuckles was loose and wrinkled, compared to his.

"You know, this reminds me of rehab," Paul said.

I groaned.

"Once in a while the inmates used to sling plates. Or worse. One time a cokehead named Stan put his fist through the TV. It's scary when people lose it like that, but they look so clear they almost shine. They look real."

"I always thought Marta expressed enough anger for the whole family."

"I like her. She's got balls."

I felt a flicker of exasperation. "And she usually leaves a big mess for somebody else to clean up."

"You don't have to clean up after her. Just be a witness. That's all she wants."

"Oh Paul, come on. You think I should let my mother clean it up? My job in this house is to take care of everybody, cover up, shut up, clean up, tiptoe around the house like a diplomat on twenty-four-hour call. If I don't do that—"

"What? What's the worst that could happen?"

"They might kill each other. Apparently my mother already has a head start," I said sharply, annoyed by his question. I pulled away from him, stood up, and walked to the window.

Paul leaned back against the gray and white stripes of the mattress, his arms behind his head. "Ever since we got here, you've been looking tight around the mouth. As if everything is your responsibility."

My exasperation grew. "Who else do you see taking it on? I'm the only one who can salvage what's left of this family."

"How long will you stay here?"

"I'm going to be here for at least a couple of weeks. Marta leaves tomorrow. I'll drive her to the airport, then try to figure out how to deal with my mother."

"Will that be a problem?"

"You can't imagine. My father did everything for her. I don't know how she's going to cope."

"Neighbors?" he asked hopefully.

"My mother has no friends. She has social alliances, mostly with people she pays. The priest, the shrink, the maid. People like that. She doesn't open up to people. And I'm sure she feels ashamed of not being able to go out, so she hides it. She doesn't want other people to know."

"You're not thinking of moving in with her, are you?"

I hesitated. "She's all alone."

"I don't like the sound of this."

"What else can I do?"

Paul sat up on the bed. "Let her work it out for herself."

"I'm not that selfish."

"Come here," Paul said, patting the bed.

I crossed my arms against my chest and leaned against the window frame, my eyes fixed on the impeccable lawn. "My mother is my responsibility now, Paul. I can't leave her."

"You think you can fix her? Lead her life for her, erase all her mistakes?"

"What would you suggest? Running away? You think that's worked for you? You've run away from your father your whole life, and it's gotten you nowhere."

"At least I know where the line is between my father and me. My father will never own me. You don't even know where that line is with your mother."

"Has it really brought you any peace of mind to run away from him? He's the only father you're ever going to have. You piss him off deliberately and then whine about him pushing you around. Why not find out who he really is, when you're not baiting him?"

"I know who he is. He's a jerk."

"He's your father, for God's sake. Some day he'll be dead." I felt a wave of fatigue wash over me, a tiredness that swept through my limbs and made them feel like lead.

"He killed my mother."

"You really believe your father has the power to give somebody cancer?" It sounded like he was just making an excuse. "If you think he killed your mother, why don't you tell him that? Have it out with him."

"You don't know what he's like."

"All I know is that your father controls you because you do exactly the opposite of what he wants. It's predictable, Paul. It's boring. You're like a hamster on a wheel, running nowhere, and your dad is at the center. You're not free. You're not even close."

Paul jumped up from the bed and stood in front of me, his eyes narrowed. "You're scared."

I laughed and put my hand to my throat. "I'm not scared." I did not want this to be about me. I wanted it to be about his inadequacy, not mine.

"You're scared of what you feel for me. You're scared of what might happen if you let go."

"Letting go is not an option here."

"It's always an option."

I shook my head and pinched the bridge of my nose between thumb and forefinger. "Paul, this is the end of the ride. I have to be a daughter here—I can't be your excuse for not working. I loved being with you. I loved the whole ride. I don't regret any of it. But I have to stay here for a while."

"So now you've gotten your rocks off, you're done with me?"

It hurt to think he could believe this. Maybe he thought I was one of those predatory older women, interested in satisfying an itch, no more than that. Maybe it would be best for both of us if he thought so.

"Something like that," I said.

He lifted an elbow and leaned it on the window frame, his hip cocked insolently toward me. He laughed a warm, pleasant, very intimate laugh. "Then let's fuck. Just for old time's sake."

"No."

"Why not? It doesn't mean anything."

I closed my eyes and felt tears spark under my eyelids. He was only calling my bluff, but the fact was that all those nights in Canyonlands, the days on the river, the walks, the conversations, the lovemaking—these memories were precious to me, and I wanted to keep them safely boxed in the past. I didn't want to forget them. But I didn't want to risk the mess, the pain of loving a younger man. Suddenly I felt ashamed, and angry that he could so quickly corner me in a lie. He didn't belong here. I didn't want him here.

The good part was over anyway. I found a flat, steady voice to speak in and used it.

"I have some errands to run after I take Marta to the airport, and I need some time here with my mother, alone. Maybe you could go into the city, see the sights, take in a Broadway show."

Paul stepped back, a patch of red on each cheek. "Don't treat me like another goddamn thing you have to fix, Zoe. I'm a big boy, I can take care of myself. If you don't want me here, I'll leave."

"I'm sorry!" I snapped at him. "You're just a little more than I can handle right now."

"Hey, no problem. I don't like being handled anyway," he said, his voice so cold it froze the air between us.

The twilight gathered around the house, a gradual darkening that felt like a stain seeping in through the doors and windows. I closed the drapes in the living room, turned on the lamp next to the sofa and sat in the pool of light. I let my head sink against the cushion and rubbed my eyes. It had been a long day. The flight had left me drained, and the reunion with my family had gone about as well as a stroll through a field full of land mines. I was exhausted.

It had been at least an hour since I'd seen Paul. Probably upstairs sulking, I thought. The hum of a car engine in the driveway shook me out of my stupor, and when I turned toward the sound, the glaze of headlights swept across the back of the curtains.

I went to the front door and opened it. A taxi was braking to a halt in front of the house, and Paul was striding to meet it, duffel bag slung over his shoulder.

"Wait!" I called.

Paul turned and waited for me to speak. The

deepening twilight was so dim he was little more than a silhouette. I couldn't see his expression, but I was reluctant to go closer, to see what this meant.

"Where are you going?" I asked.

"Does it matter?" he asked. His voice was cold.

"Can you leave me a number where I can reach you?"

"You can't have it both ways, Zoe." He opened the rear door and threw his bag inside.

"I don't want you to leave like this."

"Why? Isn't this what you wanted?"

What could I say? Wasn't this exactly what I'd asked for? He was right. I couldn't have it both ways, but now that he was leaving I felt a sharp ache swell in my chest, as if a splinter had driven itself into my heart. It was over.

I stood there, frustrated, boxed in by my own warring emotions, afraid to go toward him, afraid to let him go.

He muttered something to the driver and darted back toward the house, moving so quickly I stood frozen, rooted to the landing. As he rushed closer the glow from the window lit his face, and I could see the rage in his twisted expression.

I was certain he was going to hit me. I

flinched and lifted one arm to cover my face. With one hand he yanked mine down and pinned it behind me, and with his other hand he circled my waist and pressed me against the column.

He kissed me, hard.

It was a savage kiss, a rape, not a caress. I could feel his teeth grind against my bottom lip, his tongue thrust deep in my mouth while his arms squeezed the air out of my lungs. I was terrified and aroused in the same moment, but above all I was angry. My first instinct had been correct: he wanted to hurt me.

He let me go as abruptly as he'd seized me, shoved me away without a word, ran down the steps, jumped in the back seat of the cab, and slammed the door.

I watched, stunned, as the taxi rolled down the drive. My lips were bruised and my breathing was shallow, rapid. Don't cry, I told myself. If you let yourself cry you'll fall apart. Slowly, deliberately, as if it were an assignment from my father, I took one deep breath and then another. Everything would be all right. This was all for the best. I wasn't dead, and the world would go on spinning.

Ten

I drove Marta to Kennedy Airport in Richard's Lincoln.

"I liked him," Marta said. "That Paul kid."

I kept my mouth firmly shut.

"Where'd he go?"

"I don't know."

"I bet he was great in bed."

"He's eleven years younger than I am."

"Yeah, that helps."

"That's not what I meant," I said.

"He doesn't seem to mind. Do you?"

"Yes, frankly. Sooner or later he would, too."

"Why not cross that bridge when you get to it?"

I gave my sister a sardonic look.

"You don't have to tie up every relationship into a nice legal knot, you know. Aren't you ready for something else?"

"No."

"Oh, loosen up, for Christ's sake."

As if it were that easy, I thought. I didn't want to think about Paul anymore, I wanted to freeze the part of myself that ached with loss and feel something else. It was only ten o'clock in the morning and I already felt like I'd been run over.

"Did you say good-bye to Mom?" I asked.

Marta stared listlessly out the window.

"Did you?" I prodded.

Marta turned to face me. I was struck again by the shadows under her eyes, the puffy red rims, the bruised look of grief.

"I hate her," Marta said.

I started to speak, then shrugged.

"I do," Marta insisted.

"Do you think she can go on living in the house all by herself?" I asked.

"Beats me."

"Don't you think we should figure out something? She wouldn't even come out of her room last night."

"Let her deal with it."

"I could move in with her."

"Ha!" Marta said flatly. "I should have known you'd come up with some great excuse to martyr yourself again."

"What's that supposed to mean?"

"You get off on sacrificing yourself. You did it in your marriage and you're ready to do it now."

It seemed the conversation had suddenly switched to another topic without warning. "I liked being married. More or less."

"Why? All you did was tiptoe around Jake like he was the emperor of the universe. You were never equal to him. He was just like Dad. Both of them fucked around. Both of them acted like they deserved to be waited on hand and foot."

"It wasn't like that at all," I protested.

"Why did you believe that phony shit they pulled? Who died and made them king? Whenever Dad came home you jumped out of his chair like it was his throne."

I drove for a while in silence. Beneath the canopy of maples light danced across the hood of my father's blue Lincoln. I signaled a left and cruised through downtown Westport, passing seafood restaurants, real estate offices, bookshops, cafes, and bakeries selling croissants and expensive coffee. Marta shook out a cigarette, lit it, and exhaled the smoke out the window.

I sniffed. "I'm surprised you care so much

about the way he died. You sound like you hated him."

"Hey, it surprises the shit out of me. What can I do? It's just so fucking sad. Now I'll never get another chance with him. I feel like I lost some piece of the future that I didn't even know I was counting on."

I was quiet for a moment, then spoke. "When I was four or five years old he came home from work one day and crouched on the floor to give me a hug. 'How's my girl?' he said. He tried to hold me but I struggled and pushed him away. I wouldn't let him pick me up. You're a liar, I thought. You act like you love us but you're gone all the time and when you're home you can't wait to leave."

Marta stubbed out her cigarette, and I could see the shine of tears on her cheek as she leaned forward.

I went on. "He looked so hurt, and then he covered the hurt with a smile. I was too little to know how powerful that moment would become. That was when I locked him out of my heart, and he knew it. I never let him back in."

"You were just a little girl," Marta said. "You were being loyal to Mom."

"Still. I wish I'd hugged him back then. I wish I could hug him now."

We fell into an awkward silence. I watched the signs for the Connecticut thruway.

"You know, the car still smells like Dad," I said, accelerating to merge with the traffic.

"Old Spice." Marta suddenly giggled. "And his farts."

"I bet his flask is still in the glove compartment," I said.

Marta pushed the recessed button and opened it. "So it is," she said. "Want a little snort?" She unscrewed the top of the flask and held it out to me.

"To Dad," I said, tilting the monogrammed silver container to take a long swallow. My eyes burned. The taste of gin always gave me a sharp sensory memory of my father. His smile over the rim of a glass. The smell of starch and laundry soap in his shirts, his tenor voice singing "Ain't Misbehavin' " with the radio.

Marta took a nip. "Tanqueray," she announced.

"He might have waved the vermouth bottle over the flask," I said, imitating my father's drawl. We looked at each other and burst out laughing.

"He was a *drunk*," Marta gasped.

"Ah, poor Dad," I agreed, laughing helplessly. "He was a drunk."

* * *

When I returned from the airport, Amelia was in the kitchen, buttering a piece of toast.

"Hi, Mom," I said.

Amelia dropped the knife and whirled around, her hand touching her throat. "I thought you'd all left."

"The others did. I'll be here for a few days."

Amelia turned back to the counter and picked up the knife. "There's really no need. I don't want to inconvenience you."

Only my mother would speak like this, I thought, as if death were no more than an inconvenience. "I'm a little concerned about you."

"But why? Surely you have your own life to worry you. The divorce, the loss of your job . . ."

"I didn't lose my job, Mom; I chose to leave. And I chose the divorce."

"Of course you did, dear. It just seems to me that you should be spending your time on other things, not fretting about your mother. I'll be fine."

"Can you leave the house?" I asked bluntly.

Amelia's face froze, as if she'd been caught in a lie. "Leave the house?"

"Yes. Leave the house. Go out the door and stand in the garden. Can you do that?"

Amelia reached into the cabinet for a jar of

preserves. The only sound in the kitchen was the hum of the refrigerator and her knife scraping over the toast. When she finished spreading the jam, she laid the knife in the sink and spoke with her back to me.

"I know you're anxious about me, Zoe, but I find it uncomfortable. You really don't have to take care of me. I've made plans of my own."

"What plans? How can you have plans if you can't step out the door?"

When Amelia turned around her face looked pinched, affronted. She put the top on the butter dish and brushed the crumbs off her hands.

"You aren't going to miss Dad at all, are you?" I asked.

Amelia pursed her lips and considered her toast with an air of judicious detachment. "Of course, I'll miss certain things. But your father and I led very separate lives under this roof. I'm sure you knew that."

"Are you saying it really doesn't matter to you that he's dead?"

"I believe in the immortality of the soul, Zoe."

"I see. Why bother grieving, then? It all fits into the divine plan, right?"

"That's not what I meant."

"Mom, I can't help but wonder if he'd still be alive if you had the courage to go outside."

"I know Marta believes that. I don't blame you if you choose to believe it, too."

"Give me one reason why I shouldn't."

Amelia picked up her plate and smiled graciously at me, as if we were discussing the weather. "I'll be in my room," she said.

I moved around the house, restless as a caged dog. I wanted a fight, and my mother refused to cooperate. On impulse I lifted the phone receiver in the kitchen and punched out the number for information in Petaluma, California. The operator gave me the number for Paul's father. After drumming my nails a few times on the counter, I called the number.

"Hello?"

"Mr. Griffin?"

"Yes?"

"My name is Zoe Harper. I'm a friend of your son's."

"Ah."

"Paul and I traveled together for a few weeks and then I lost touch with him. I'm trying to locate him again. Do you have a number where he can be reached?"

"What would this be regarding?"

Good question, I thought. "I guess you could say this is a social call."

"Are you the woman who called me before about the money he left in your vehicle?"

"Yes, that's right. Paul met me the morning after I spoke with you and convinced me to take him to Montana."

"How on earth did he persuade you to take him to Montana?" Mr. Griffin sounded amused.

"I saw the bruises on his face."

The amusement vanished. "Yes, I see." There was a pause, as if he were debating with himself about whether or not to continue the conversation. "That was a terrible night."

"He said you and he had a fight about the money, and you were planning to confiscate it."

"No. The money is Paul's. I would never force him to give it to me."

"He told me a different story."

Mr. Griffin coughed. The silence thickened between us, and I refused to break it.

Finally he spoke. "We argued for hours that night. All that cash—it seemed outrageous to me that he could treat his mother's inheritance so callously. Before she died, it was one of the most productive portfolios I'd ever managed. A good chunk of it was in Fidelty Investment's Magellan Fund, which paid one hundred and forty percent over the past five years. You can't even buy into that fund anymore."

"Surely it was up to him what he did with the money, not you."

"I just couldn't understand it. I was afraid for him. I tried to persuade him to leave the money where it was, and he began shouting at me. We almost came to blows. It was my fault that he tripped. I was angry, but I never meant to hurt him."

"If you know where he is, I'd be grateful if you'd tell me."

There was a sigh, and when he spoke his voice wobbled. "I don't know where he is. I might ask the same of you, if you hear from him. I'm worried."

"Why? Has anything happened? Did he call you?"

"He called yesterday. He sounded upset. He said something about his mother that I found very disturbing. He thinks I caused her death somehow, although I can't fathom the connection."

"He said something like that to me, once." My face flushed, and I could feel the warmth creep into my scalp. I hoped Paul hadn't mentioned it was my idea for him to confront his father.

"I know her death must be a shock to him," he said.

"He's still grieving."

"Everyone who ever met my wife loved her. She could light up a room with her smile. She was the bridge between me and Paul, and when she died—" he stopped talking. I let the silence blossom between us.

He cleared his throat and went on. "It was the worst thing I ever went through. Paul was so hurt, but I couldn't comfort him. I was angry. I hated the couples I saw in the street, holding hands. I lashed out at Paul, I said things—"

Again he was silent, and I could hear the muffled, terrible sound of his weeping.

"I'm so sorry," I said.

"I love my son, Ms. Harper. I love him. I want him to know that. He's all I have left of her."

"I know," I said.

"Please, I need to talk to him. If you hear from him, let me know."

"I will," I promised. "I'd like it if you'd do the same for me."

I hung up the phone and stared out the kitchen window, into the backyard. There was nothing I could do for Paul's father. My hands ached with helplessness. There was nothing I could do for Paul, or my mother, or myself.

Nothing but serene views everywhere, I thought sourly. The lawn sloped off from the terrace, and a break in the trees at the perimeter of the property allowed a glimpse of Long Island Sound in the blue distance.

I stalked out the door and crossed the flagstone terrace to the old carriage house that served as a garden shed. The latch on the door lifted easily and the door swung open on silent, well-oiled hinges. When I stepped into the cool darkness I felt like an intruder. This was the heart of my father's territory. Weak shafts of light filtered through dusty glass windows, and the smell of earth and grass and machine oil hung in the air. His gardening tools were neatly arranged on hooks in pegboard, and a variety of mowers and tillers were parked along the north wall.

In the chill of the room my mind simmered like a pot about to boil over. The house had locked my mother up like Rapunzel. My father's death unlocked nothing. I selected a shovel and hefted it in my hand, testing the weight. The hardwood grip was smooth with use. A coiled garden hose sat under the workbench and I pulled it out, shook the last few drops of water from the nozzle, and slung the hose over my shoulder.

Outside the air was clear and blue and unusually hot even for early June. A pair of orioles chased each other from the trellis to the ash tree shading the driveway. As I walked around the house I could see there were people out on the street: on one of the wide lawns farther down the hill two little kids were throwing a big pink plastic ball back and forth, and an old man was walking his dalmatian on the sidewalk. I went past the flowerbeds to stand in the center of the wide front lawn. Gauging the distance between the house and the street, I adjusted my position for maximum visibility.

The velvet stretch of clipped Kentucky bluegrass sloped directly down to the sidewalk in an unbroken expanse of green. There were no dandelions, no rosettes of crabgrass to mar the emerald carpet that stretched out like a fairway before me. The front lawn had always been my father's special pride, and in the last few years of his life he'd been obsessed with its perfection. It didn't surprise me at all that he died for a dandelion. He'd always had a crew of gardeners for the trees and the wide flowerbeds, but he attended to the needs of the front lawn himself.

I picked up the shovel, placed the blade against the dense, thick mat of sod, braced myself with my right foot and pressed down on the shovel with my left. The ground was soft from the late spring rains, and the grass roots broke easily as the metal bit into the soil. Tossing a shovelful of earth off to the side, I dug again into the broken turf.

The front door opened a few inches. "Zoe!" my mother hissed from the portico. "What are you doing?"

"I'm making something for you," I said, stabbing the lawn again.

"I don't want anything," my mother said, her voice rising.

"I know, Mom. I'm making it for you anyway," I said flatly.

The topsoil was scrupulously groomed, ten inches of black, fertile dirt, with hardly any pebbles to mar its texture. A light mineral odor floated up as I bore down into the compacted earth. Underneath the cultivated topsoil the dirt paled to gray, and my shovel hit rocks the size of potatoes. The stubborn clay weighed heavily on the blade, clinging when I tried to toss the load aside.

All afternoon I attacked the hole, and when the number of rocks made it impossible to use the shovel, I went back to the carriage house for a pickax. It took a few attempts to get the rhythm right, but soon my arms swung the heavy pick high above my head. Over and over, I slammed the blade into the earth.

The paperboy came riding up on his bike, his eyes thrilled. He gave me the paper and I tossed it aside, my grimy hands smearing the print. We looked at each other and smiled. When he pedaled away he popped a wheelie.

The rocks were larger two feet down, big as bowling balls. One was huge, the size of a watermelon. I sat with my legs on both sides of it and scraped the dirt away with my hands. When I could see the hard slope of the stone curving under, I pried it free with the shovel, then lifted it out by hand.

After three hours of digging I stood up and pressed my fists into the small of my back, nursing the ache. I was out of breath as I looked at my hole. It was six feet across and four feet deep. It was probably big enough.

The lawn was ruined. The hole looked like a bomb crater. Piles of dirt and rocks and clumps of mangled sod were heaped everywhere around it. I sat down and began breaking up the clods with my hands, pushing the loose soil back in the hole, shoving the roots and rocks aside. The task absorbed me, and I felt a certain sense of accomplishment as my hands sifted the earth.

When I finished there was a mound of soft dirt in the hole. I walked to the side of the house to connect the hose to the faucet, then turned it on. The gushing hose directed a stream of water into the pit. Propping the hose on the edge of the hole, I stirred the water into the dirt with my shovel until I had a deep well of puddinglike mud. The clay bed held the water trapped like a pond.

The smell of the earth reminded me of mixing adobe for our house in Santa Fe ten years ago. Back then it had been a smell that meant hours of lifting and plastering. Jake and I slaved for fourteen months to get the inner and outer surface of the house just right.

Now the smell of water filling the hole reminded me of making love to Paul by the river. People are clear when they're angry, Paul said yesterday. They look real. I felt real. Even though my arms burned and my legs shook when I stood up, my whole body was energized by the destruction of my father's turf. I felt powerful, like a witch about to break a spell.

I wiped the sweat from my forehead with the back of my hand. The hole was ready. Now comes the hard part, I thought.

"No," my mother said.

"You can do this, Mom," I said.

"I will not. You're insane."

I almost laughed at the accusation as I considered the source. "Just stand in the doorway. I'll help you."

Amelia looked at me distrustfully. "Dr. Daniels told me not to rush into anything," she said.

"Mom, you haven't been outside in thirty years. I don't think you could call this rushing things."

"I know you blame me for Richard's death," she said plaintively, resisting my unsubtle pressure on her arm.

"Marta does. I don't," I said. We had worked our way down the hallway to the wide front door, the edge of my mother's world.

"Open it," I said.

"Promise you won't push me," she said, her breathing shallow and panicky.

"I promise," I said.

Amelia opened the door and swayed on the threshold. "What a lovely day," she said weakly.

"I'm right here, Mom. Just one more step."

"Don't push me," she said.

"I won't."

Amelia stepped out on the welcome mat. She squinted up at the bright June sky. "I don't feel well at all," she said.

"Take a deep breath."

"I think I'll go back in now."

"Okay."

"It's very hot, isn't it?"

"Yes, it is."

"I can smell the grass," my mother said, fainting into a graceful heap at my feet.

The next day I watered the hole again. The sediment had settled, leaving a grayish-brown watery puddle on top, but as I stirred it with my shovel the mud achieved a satiny, homogenized texture. I dipped my fingers into the muck. It felt cool, just the right temperature for the day. It was going to be another scorcher.

In the furthest corner of my peripheral vision I could see the front door was cracked open.

"Ready, Mom?" I called out, my eyes on the shovel as I stirred the mud in the pit.

The door clicked shut.

I looked up at the hot, pale sky. "Help me, Dad," I said in a conversational voice.

We were wedged in the doorway again, my mother's hands clutching the doorframe. I was surprised at the strength in Amelia's frail body. Sometimes I was tempted to knee her in the back and shove, but I doubted I could break her death grip on the front door.

"Dr. Daniels has me work with visualization," my mother explained patiently. "I imagine going through the door. I'm very good at it. He says I've made tremendous progress."

"How much do you pay him?" I asked.

"Don't be vulgar."

"Ready?"

"No, I—"

I noticed that her hand had relaxed slightly on the doorframe. I moved to take her hand in my own.

"I'm right here," I said.

My mother's eyes wavered in panic, her breathing hoarse and uneven.

"Look at me," I said, braced to catch her if she fell. I looked into Amelia's frightened face and for a brief moment I saw my own eyes looking back at me, full of terror. That look—it was so familiar, so recent. When had I felt such paralyzed fear? The memory flashed over my skin and sent a chill through me: the night of the storm, when I saw Paul disappear in the river.

Suddenly I knew exactly how my mother felt, knew it required more than courage for her to stand on her own threshold.

"I love you, Mom," I said, still holding her hand.

Her face relaxed slightly. "Okay," she said. "I'm ready."

We staggered out together, and a moment later we were both standing by the hole. Amelia was weaving like a drunk. I kept my arm around her waist, but it was tricky maintaining a balance for both of us.

"Look what you did to Richard's lawn," Amelia said breathlessly.

"Why don't you sit here for a minute?"

"My dress will get dirty," she said, sagging to the grass by the edge of the hole.

"Here, hold this," I said, handing her the hose.

"Oh, I can't . . . what are you doing?"

I unbuttoned my shirt, unzipped my shorts and stripped down to my bathing suit. The air was hot and humid, and the sluggish breeze offered little relief. I extended one leg into the hole and swirled my foot in the mud to test the temperature. With a sigh of satisfaction I slid into the hole, bending my knees until the cool muck covered my shoulders. I looked up at my mother.

Amelia was blinking up at the sky, her eyes slitted in the harsh light, a dreamy expression on her face. "I'm outside," she said. Her voice was faint.

I crawled quickly out of the hole, my limbs black. "Mom, spray me," I said.

Amelia looked dazed, her body quivering like a dog in a thunderstorm. I pointed to the spray nozzle my mother held in her lap. She picked it up, pulled the trigger, and sent a torrent of water into the air. The droplets came down like hard rain on both of us. Amelia looked mildly surprised, then more focused and serious as she aimed the nozzle at me. I turned around under the spray.

The water was colder than I thought it would be. I stood still for as long as I could and looked out at the street, where trees and cars and houses were veiled in small circular rainbows. When I turned around to face my mother, Amelia's hair was luminous, sparkling in the spray of shattered light.

"All right! That's enough!" I shouted.

"No, it's not," my mother argued. "You're still a mess."

That night I couldn't sleep. I was elated by my mother's progress. I didn't want to make too much of a fuss about it in front of her, because she still had a long way to go, but I was convinced I'd have her in a car by the end of the week.

I wanted to share the news with someone, but I didn't want to tell Marta until I was certain this was the beginning of a true recovery. I didn't want her to criticize my hopes.

I reached for the phone by my bed. With the three hour time difference, it was a decent hour in California. I dialed the number for Paul's father.

"Hello?"

"Mr. Griffin, it's Zoe. How are you?"

"I'm fine." His voice was cool, and I felt rebuked by the tone.

"Have you heard from Paul?"

"I have."

My heartbeat quickened. "Do you have a number where he can be reached?"

There was a pause that stretched too long to be polite.

"Paul told me about his visit to your family," he said.

"Oh." Damn, I thought.

"Under the circumstances I'm not sure it's appropriate to give you any more information."

"Look," I said, "Paul told me a number of things about you that might convince me to keep his whereabouts from you as well. But after talking to you, I think you have his best interests at heart. So do I. Can't you give me the benefit of the doubt?"

He sighed. "He asked me specifically to not tell you."

"Is he on his way to see you?" It was a guess.

"Yes."

"Could you ask him to call me? If I'm not here he can leave a message."

"All right."

"Thank you."

I told myself I just wanted to be sure he was all right. I might even apologize for anything unkind I might have said. I'd tell him I hoped we could be friends. No more than that. But I missed him with an ache that was as fierce as any I ever felt for Jake. For every thought I gave to Jake, I had a hundred for Paul.

My mother and I went out and sat by the hole every day for the rest of the week, me in it up to my neck, my mother sitting by the edge. When my legs started to cramp I got out and Amelia sprayed me with the hose.

"You're filthy!" Amelia squealed in delight every time I emerged, covered in mud.

"Let's let it dry," I suggested on the fourth day.

Amelia looked disappointed.

"You get in," I said.

My mother's lip twitched. "In my dress?" she asked wryly.

"Go get a bathing suit."

Amelia shook her head. "I don't own a bathing suit," she said.

I eyed my mother's dress critically. It was a brown plaid shirtwaist, belted and darted, thirty years out of date. She had always been thin and the dress emphasized her sticklike arms and legs. And her hair, which had been a deep chestnut brown for sixty-five years, was now bright white.

"When did you stop dyeing your hair?" I asked.

"Last year. My hairdresser used to come to the house, but she retired because of arthritis."

"Do you think you're ready to go to the beauty parlor?"

Amelia's face softened as she looked at me. "You just don't know, do you?"

"Know what?"

"What it's like for me," she said slowly, fingering the nozzle of the hose.

"I know you're scared," I said.

"It's more than that. The ground under my feet turns to molasses. My heart palpitates, I can't breathe, I can't think."

"But look where you are," I said.

"Well, yes, I'm technically outside, but the house is right there if I need it."

I reached out and carefully dotted my mother's nose with a drop of mud. "You're stronger than you think," I said.

She wiped the mud away with the back of her hand, leaving a small brown shadow.

"Why did this happen to you?" I asked, looking casually at the street as if it hadn't taken me thirty years to ask. "Was it because of those slides I showed you?"

"What slides?"

"The ones of Dad's secretary."

"Oh, those—no, not really. Although I can see how you must have thought that."

"Then what happened?"

"It's hard to explain, Zoe."

"Try."

"It was a very different world back then, in the fifties," my mother said slowly. "The bomb had just been invented. I used to wake up every morning and feel amazed that I was still alive, that we hadn't been killed in the night by Communists. Every day seemed like a gift. I expected disaster every minute, every hour. I didn't take peace for granted."

I shrugged. "So you couldn't adapt?"

Amelia smiled. "We adapted. Richard converted the cellar into a bomb shelter. There were air raid drills once a month. We lived with a paranoia that was absolutely acceptable back then."

"But most people recovered from it," I said.

"Do you think so? I wonder about that. Do you watch the news? What are we doing with all these nuclear weapons? All these handguns? We're all still ready to kill each other."

"I agree, but I go shopping. I drive. I can sit outside without panicking," I said.

Amelia nodded, averting her eyes. "I can't defend myself to you," she said, "but you did ask how this happened."

"Go on," I said, hugging my muddy knees.

"My father died, right after Marta was born. My mother went into a depression, stayed indoors, and refused to visit us. When I went to visit her she wouldn't look at me, wouldn't talk to me. She just turned her face to the wall and stayed in bed until she died too. So I was suddenly cut off from both my parents when you girls were still little."

"Is that what traumatized you?"

"Zoe, it wasn't any one thing. Richard was starting to do well at work. He was invited to parties in the city, and he wanted to rub elbows with the rich and famous. I felt so out of place whenever I went with him. It was torture for me to act witty and silly at those parties. I just wanted to go home.

"Richard was more than willing to indulge me, as I indulged him. I think he was nervous about his own infidelities. He was relieved that I didn't want to go out. He felt more secure if I stayed home, away from the scene of his crimes. So I did."

"Why didn't you divorce him?" I asked.

"I never even thought of it," my mother said simply. "Divorce was not only against my religion, it was practically unheard of back then. And you may not understand this, but I felt very happy with our arrangement."

"You're right. I don't understand."

"It took care of so many problems. I didn't have to worry about how to dress, how to invent meaningless chitchat at cocktail parties."

"You gave up your life, Mom."

"You just don't understand the life I've had."

"But you can't say you've been happy."

Amelia shook her head and took a deep breath. I felt a chill cross over me in spite of the heat.

"There is a certain peace that comes from confinement. The mind experiences an almost superhuman facility to pursue one thread of thought for days, for years. When you and Marta left, I learned how to enter a contemplative life, and I found a connection to a love I didn't expect."

"You lost me," I said blankly.

"I went back to God, Zoe."

"Oh, no," I said. "Don't tell me you're born again."

Amelia smiled. "Being born once is quite enough, I think. I was born into a family that had a strong faith. I never lost that faith. God is my truest confidant, my greatest ally. I think Richard knew that. In an odd way he was jealous because he knew he came second in my affections."

"You've spent your whole life behind these walls. Don't you wonder what kind of life you might have if you could go beyond them?"

"Zoe, I wish you wouldn't worry so much. I feel loved. I feel protected. I feel cared for, even in seclusion."

"But you didn't make a free choice. You're phobic. You're paralyzed by the thought of moving around freely in the outside world."

"What is a phobia?" my mother asked. "Isn't it merely a deeply ingrained preference? Just because you don't approve of my preference doesn't mean I have to change it."

"Aren't you glad you're out here?" I pleaded. "Doesn't the air smell sweet? Isn't it nice to feel the sun on your arms? Watch the clouds? Feel the wind in your hair?"

"Of course. I'm so grateful to have this time with you. Life brings strange gifts, and I count you as one of them."

"Then why not go shopping with me?" I asked.

Amelia's eyes crinkled. "I know you're just dying to make me over, honey."

"Why not? How many years do you have left? Do you really want to spend them shut up inside?"

"Actually, dear heart, I do."

I looked at my mother, thunderstruck with disbelief. "What?"

"Last week I called a convent in upstate New York, near Watkin's Glen; the Sisters of St. Joseph. They're a contemplative order, and I've made arrangements to go there. They've agreed to consider me as a postulant, a candidate for holy orders."

"Oh no," I said. "No, no, no."

"After a year I'll be eligible for the novitiate. In another four years I'll take my vows," Amelia continued. She placed her hand on my knee. "Please. Let me go. Get on with your life."

"You can't do this. I'll help you. I'll stay here if you want me to."

My mother smiled tenderly. "I'm not interested in the kind of life you think I should have." She looked as if she were already far away, out of reach, gone. She looked radiant.

"I want to be a nun, Zoe."

Eleven

The next morning I found my mother waiting for me at the base of the staircase, her face tense with anticipation. She looked twenty years younger, alive, ready, glowing with excitement. She had packed a single suitcase.

"That can't be all you're taking," I said.

"I have all I need."

"What about the house? What are we supposed to do with it?"

"It's already on the market. I don't want you girls to take on the maintenance for it. It's a full-time job neither of you need. The realtor's number is on the refrigerator, and when they sell it the money will be divided equally between you and Marta. If there's any furniture you want, take it. Otherwise they've been instructed to sell the contents with the house."

"Do you have money?"

"Of course. Richard left quite a bit of cash, as well as stocks and bonds. I'm giving most of the cash to the convent. I don't know if they could afford to accept me without it."

"Are you sure this is what you want?" It seemed incredible to me that my mother could walk away from me now that I was willing to devote my energy to making her well.

"I've waited so long to do this, Zoe." A kind of anguish crossed her face, and she bit her lip and reached out to clasp me in a fierce hug. "Don't wait so long to live the life you want," she whispered in my ear.

She released me from the hug but let her hands remain on my shoulders and gave me a little shake, as if to emphasize her words. "I'll never regret the life I had with your father, because it gave me you and Marta. You've been a gift to me. Don't ever doubt that." She smoothed the hair back from my forehead and I had to shut my eyes against a grief that threatened to overwhelm me.

"We'd better get going, or I won't be able to do this," I said, lifting her suitcase. "I'll come back to walk you to the car."

The morning was clear, the intense heat held at bay, and the sky had lost its film of haze. The hole looked foolish, a relic of another ruined hope I'd have to clean up later. I unlocked the trunk of Richard's Lincoln, put the suitcase inside and turned to go back up the walk for my mother.

She was already standing outside the door. She held her hand up, palm out, to stop me from coming back for her.

"I want to do this by myself," she said.

She'd never attempted to walk outside without me, but now she edged her way cautiously across the landing. At the first step she stopped, but when I started to move toward her she waved me back.

She cautiously extended one foot out to explore the space above the first step. I held my breath and nodded encouragement. It took her about thirty seconds to get one foot securely planted on the second step. Another minute and a half went by before she brought her other foot down. It took an eternity for her to descend all four steps, but when she finally reached the sidewalk she laughed with relief. It seemed as grand an accomplishment as a parachute jump. I applauded as she continued down the walkway, wobbling her way toward me.

The drive went quickly. We were silent for most of it, and I was glad she didn't want to talk. I was jealous of her certainty, her faith in the future, her courage, and I was ashamed to be jealous of her. She had a plan and the nerve to carry it out. In comparison, my life felt as raw, empty, and ugly as the hole in the lawn.

With every mile my mother seemed to gather energy. Her face was rosy, her breathing deliberately deep. When I merged with the traffic on the freeway she closed her eyes and I was jolted by the realization that this was the first time she'd been driven anywhere in thirty years. This was her first freeway.

"Are you okay?" I asked when I saw her close her eyes. She nodded, and I kept going.

When we arrived at the convent we were met at the gate by a nun dressed in the long black skirt, veil, and wimple of the traditional habit.

"I'm so glad to meet you, Mrs. Harper," she said to my mother. "I'm Sister Joan of Arc. We have your room ready for you. Is this your daughter?"

"Zoe," I said and nodded. I wasn't sure whether or not to offer my hand for her to shake. When I stole a glance at my mother I saw she kept her hands demurely clasped, so I did the same.

"I'm afraid this is as far as you can go, Zoe," the nun said. For a moment I wasn't sure what she meant. How far could I go? Surely I could go anywhere I wanted.

"We're a cloistered community," she explained. "Outsiders aren't permitted on the grounds except once a year, on visiting day. We'll be sending you a newsletter to announce those times."

I looked at my mother in shock and she smiled.

"I'll get your bag," I said, to cover my confusion.

My mother waited silently with the nun while I unlocked the trunk and lifted the bag. Sister Joan of Arc took the suitcase and walked a few steps up the drive before she turned to wait for my mother.

"Good-bye," Amelia said and gave me a quick kiss on the cheek. "I'll write whenever I can." She gave my arm one last squeeze and turned and walked through the gate, her head held high, her shoulders braced for what might come. I saw her reach Sister Joan of Arc and take her arm, and then the high stone walls blocked my view of her progress. Within a moment, she was gone.

When I returned to the house it was dark. The air inside was stale, the silence heavy. I closed the drapes, poured myself a large brandy, and thought about sitting in my father's chair in the living room, but couldn't. The house seemed dead, unwelcoming, and I felt like a trespasser.

For the first time in days I realized I was free to do whatever I liked. It should have been a good feeling, but I felt cheated by the absence of my parents, angry that I'd been abandoned by both of them. I wandered into the kitchen, turned on all the lights, opened the refrigerator, and shut it again without registering any of the contents. I picked up the phone to call Marta, then changed my mind and put the receiver back in the cradle. I didn't want to rehash the last few days for her, or hear her gleeful reaction to the sudden departure of our mother.

I picked up the phone again and dialed the number for Paul's father. There was no answer. I let it ring twenty times, but no machine came on to take my message. It felt personal, somehow, another rejection, another blank wall for me to fling myself against. I took a gulp of brandy and let my resentments simmer. The brandy burned in my stomach. It had been a long day, and I couldn't remember eating anything. I'd felt like a robot during the drive to the convent and back, and hunger was a distant memory.

I opened the bread drawer, pulled out a bag of whole wheat bread, untwisted the wire that kept it closed, took out a piece of bread and ate it. It tasted like paper. I washed it down with brandy and grimaced at the taste. Eating to survive, I thought. I remember this.

I thought of the meals Paul had made for me, how he'd build a charcoal fire in a hand-dug hole and wait for the heat to become steady enough to bake chicken or potatoes wrapped in foil. I thought of the first time he cooked for me, producing figs stuffed with pesto from the tiny stove in the Winnebago. I groaned out loud, and the sound frightened me as it echoed in the sterile silence of the house. It was the sound of a crazy woman, the sound of loss.

In the morning I walked out, impatient to escape the house. I wanted to find another landscape, another view, one to match my mood: the sound of demolition, the harsh growl of bulldozers. A wrecking ball swinging into a tall brick building would do nicely.

The curving, ladylike avenues of the spacious older neighborhoods led me toward the streets in town. For a week now the temperatures had soared into the nineties every afternoon. The roads were empty in the bright heat, and leaves hung on the trees like limp pieces of cloth. When I looked at my feet they seemed far away, padding along the sidewalks of my childhood.

St. Mark's cemetery was up ahead; I'd been walking for hours and had come farther than I thought. Tall wrought iron gates guarded the tombs, and the black metal was hot on my fingers as I pushed the gate open and entered the graveyard.

It was easy to find the slab that covered my father's body. It was the freshest grave in the small cemetery. A seam of dirt lay between the marble and the broken sod, and a wilted arrangement of lilies and roses towered over it. The perfume of the flowers covered the stone like a blanket.

Feeling lightheaded, I read the beveled letters that spelled out my father's name. The marker was low on the ground, no larger than a pillow next to the bed of marble that covered his body. A drop of sweat ran down my face. I leaned down to touch his name, then lowered myself until I was sitting on the stone bed. A minute went by. Nothing stirred in the pale heat. The sky was empty as a blank sheet of paper. Stretching out on my back, I lay full length across the cool, glassy surface of the marble.

I peered up into the haze. After a week in

Montana the sky in Connecticut looked small and crowded with trees. The air was like glue. Rolling over on my belly, I pressed my cheek to the marble and stared into a line of ants working the loose soil.

"Is it cool down there?" I whispered into the grave.

I couldn't imagine that his body was under me. It seemed impossible that someone so vivid in my mind could disappear into the ground. His eyes still seemed to follow me.

A voice above me spoke out, clear and loud.

"Can I help you, miss?"

I turned, startled. A gardener looked down at me, his voice brisk and loud and suspicious. He carried a shovel in one hand, a burlap sack in the other. His face was shaded by a hat, his features obscured by the backlighting of the sun.

"No," I said, rolling over to lean on one elbow and look up at him.

"You're not sick?" he asked, his voice stern with implication, as though he were certain I was drunk or crazy or both.

"This is my father's grave," I said, letting my head drop to the stone.

"Richard was your father?" the gardener asked.

"You knew him?"

"I knew him."

I sat up and squinted to see the face under the straw hat. He was old, in his eighties at least.

"Who are you?" I asked.

"You wouldn't recognize my name," the man said. "Richard used to come to my greenhouse. I grow orchids."

"In Westport?" I asked.

"No, Easton." He gave me the first glimmer of a smile. "You must be Zoe."

I stood, wiped my hands on the back of my shorts, and offered him my hand. "That's right."

"Peter." He bent stiffly to place the sack at his feet, then took my hand. His hand was hard, leathery, and warm.

"How well did you know my father?"

Peter took off his hat and mopped his forehead with a bandana. "Well enough to miss him. He used to come and see me every Thursday afternoon. We'd have coffee, talk a bit. He seemed lonely, somehow. I was too, that's a fact. My wife died five years ago and I still miss her."

"I'm glad he had a friend."

"He was a lovely young man, your father. I met him at a nursery. We were both filching seeds from a stand of delphinium. I lent him a Baggie. I don't usually mess with common ornamentals but the seed pods were so ripe neither one of us could resist. Anyway the groundsman caught us and turned us out. We went to a shop round the corner, had tea, and talked plants for an hour."

"I thought he was more of a lawn man," I said.

"Lawns? I can't say as we ever talked lawns. No use for lawns, myself. Greedy stuff, grass. Takes over the flowers. Creates a monopoly for itself. Boring. No, your father had a high regard for beauty."

"I suppose he did," I said.

"You should have seen him in my garden. The first branch of forsythia to bloom in April was enough to stop him in his tracks. 'Look at that!' he'd say. 'The Goddess returns.' 'What Goddess are you on about?' I'd say, and he'd laugh. 'Primavera!' he'd say, and clap me on the back."

Peter scratched the whiskers on his chin, his eyes bemused and distant. "The way he talked! I always thought he could have been a writer. He could string words together like he was painting a picture. You could see what he was describing just as clear as day. I loved to listen to him."

I nodded, felt a dull ache squeeze my chest.

Peter's expression became solemn. "He was always going on about you girls. When you moved to New Mexico he suffered terribly."

"I didn't think he cared one way or the other," I said.

"He was afraid to show his tenderness, like most of us. Fathers wear the armor in this world. The armor gets awful heavy, though. I was glad he could put it down for a bit, with me."

"Well," I said, wanting to end the conversation.

Peter gestured to the bundle at his feet. "Would you help me plant this lilac? He was fond of the scent. I thought he'd like it if I—"

"Of course," I said. "It's very kind of you."

He smiled, offering me the shovel. "That's the spot, near the headstone," he said, pointing.

I took the shovel, walked behind the marker, braced my sneaker on the rim of the blade, and pushed into the soft soil. By now it was a familiar movement. I felt an abrupt awareness of the shovel lessening the distance between my foot and my father's body. I thought of Richard's face. When he was happy his eyes narrowed and the crease in the middle of his forehead was erased. There had been a lively joy in his eyes, once. Now his eyes would be closed, as if he were sleeping. But this was not sleeping.

The old man stood by, watching as I paused to blot the sweat on my forehead with the back of my arm.

"Is this deep enough?"

He looked in and shook his head. "No. Roots need a lot of space. Shall I take over?"

"No," I said, though I felt dizzy. I dug deeper, and each thrust pierced me with the irrational fear that my shovel would hit the coffin.

"That's good," Peter said. I scrambled out of the hole and stood to one side while he untied the burlap from the root ball. He put the bush into the ground gently, his gnarled hands separating the roots and pressing them delicately into place.

I stood with the shovel and watched as he sifted the soil through his fingers and tossed aside a few pebbles and an old gum wrapper. He patted the dirt around the bottom of the bush, his touch as competent and tender as a father putting a baby to bed.

A lump came to my throat as I watched Peter's hands press the soil around the stems, and my eyes filmed over with tears. When I was five or six I had pneumonia and ran a high fever for days. My father came home early from work every day to visit my room. The blinds were drawn, the windows closed. I was barely conscious, lost in the delirium of illness, and my throat was so sore I couldn't talk.

Smoothing the hair back from my forehead, cradling my cheek with his cool hand, he would whisper to me. "Think of the ocean, Zoe. Think of all that blue water, and the wind blowing over you, so cool and lovely. The air smells like salt and seaweed and it feels so fresh in your face. When you're all better we'll go down to the shore. We'll swim in the cool waves for as long as you want, and I'll carry you on my shoulders when you get tired."

A fierce pain welled up in my chest, enveloping me in terror. My father was dead, down there, in a steel box, under the ground.

I crumpled to the side of the grave and buried my face in my hands. Tears flooded my eyes and slid down my cheeks as I let the pain wash over me. Nothing could fix this. Nothing could ever fill this hole.

Peter wiped his hands on his overalls and turned toward me as if I were just another bush in the garden, another living thing in need of attention. He placed his hand on my head and held it there while I sobbed against his leg. Standing still as an oak, his feet planted wide apart, he kept his hand on the crown of my head and didn't speak.

I cried as if I were dying, as if the whole world had become strange and unbearable. It was shocking to me, how much I loved my father. I had stored up good deeds to be worthy of him, to make him love me back. Even in the past year, small things like weeding the vegetable garden or getting the oil changed in my car were imbued with the hope that these offerings would be taken into account and weigh in my favor someday. For years and years my eager heart had paced around the edge of the distance between us, looking for a place to get across.

I pushed my head against the rough fabric of the old man's trousers and hung on his leg to steady myself as the tears dripped down my face. Peter gave me the bandana from his pocket and I blew my nose and wiped my face as the misery ebbed from my body, leaving me limp and alive.

"Good girl," Peter said, still holding my head. His hand felt comforting and heavy as it cradled my skull. I felt as planted as the lilac. My lungs unlocked and air poured into my body.

I stood up then and wordlessly hugged the old man.

"He loved you," he said.

"I know."

Dark clouds had moved in from the east. The atmosphere was heavy with heat and charged air as I walked toward my mother's house. Lightning cracked in the unnatural dusk of the heavy clouds, and the rain began to fall in a steady vertical pattering. The wind lifted and a paper cup rattled toward me as it skidded down the street. Drops began to sprinkle my hot skin.

It grew into a gentle, obstinate rain, a steady rush of water that made a lush racket in the leaves, then gathered quickly in the gutters and ran beside the sidewalk. The air was thick with the benevolent odor of water and grass and wet streets. My shirt was dark with wet, plastered to my back and chest as I lifted my face to the low clouds and let the cold drops run over my face and down my collar.

Thunder rumbled across the sky. I slowed to a halt and stood without moving as the sound echoed above the trees. Holding my hands out like cups, I watched my palms fill with water. The rain fell everywhere, avoiding nothing, choosing everything, and for some reason that fact made me want to laugh out loud. It was free to anyone who held their palms upturned, another strange gift from the heavens. In the hard pelting downpour I felt washed clean of expectations, the ones I thought I had to fulfill and the ones I hoped others would take care of for me. My father's death had set me loose and cast me into a strange and overwhelming sea of possibility. I could do whatever I wanted. No one was watching anymore.

My hair and skin and clothes were soaked, but I walked without hurry through the downpour. All my life I had struggled to achieve some mysterious goal that would finally be enough, and the habit of striving was so deeply ingrained that I wasn't even sure I could stop. But there was no task to complete. The part of myself that was exhausted from trying so hard to be good could come down from the invisible cross I'd been nailed to all my life.

As I walked back to my mother's house I didn't know what the future would hold, but I knew Amelia didn't need me anymore. There was no reason to blame her for that. It was time to go.

That night I looked out my bedroom window at the gaping wound I'd inflicted on the lawn. The hole looked like an open grave for every scheme, every strategy I'd ever concocted.

Moonlight turned the grass a cold blue and the hole stared back at me like an eye, offering no answers and no apologies.

My eyes wandered around my old bedroom. It was almost empty of furniture, in contrast to the heavy Victorian decor in the rest of the house. White lace curtains covered the windows now. When I was in high school the curtains were blue, the walls were blue, the rugs were blue. Now everything was white: the duvet, the bureau, the walls, the louvered closet doors, and the lacquered frame on a Degas lithograph above the bed.

All the memorabilia of diaries, sketchbooks, yearbooks, my first clumsy paintings, the old board games, dolls, stuffed toys, and knick-knacks of childhood, even my old clothes had vanished. My mother had probably thrown them all out by now. The room was empty of me—it could be anyone's room. The person I had become had grown over and beyond my room and my family, the way a tree will seal over a strand of barbed wire, given enough time. It wasn't such a bad thing, to have that hard history inside me.

I missed Paul.

If I shut my eyes I could imagine the weight of his chin on my shoulder and the firm grip of his arms around my waist. Why am I ashamed of loving him? I asked the wall. There was no one left to judge me for it. What was it my mother had said? "Life brings strange gifts, and I count you as one of them." I knew exactly what she meant.

In my white room, the curtains rose and fell like the chest of someone sleeping. I lay on the bed and watched squares of light from a passing car tilt and climb across the walls. The phone glowed on the table by the bed, and I reached over to pick up the receiver. After dialing the number for Paul's father's house in Petaluma, I waited for an answer.

"Hello?"

"Mr. Griffin?"

"Yes?"

"It's Zoe."

"Zoe. I'm glad you called."

"Is Paul there?"

"He is. Hang on a moment, I'll get him."

"Hello?" It was his voice.

My mouth was open but I couldn't make any sound come out of it.

"It's me," I finally said.

"Oh. Hi."

His voice was cool, cautious. I opened my mouth to speak, to plunge past the deliberate silence, but there were too many things to say, too many ways to say them, and I closed my mouth again.

"Are you still there?" he asked.

"Yes. I'm here. Are you okay?"

"Uh-huh," he said.

"I didn't expect you to be at your dad's house. I was just calling to see if he'd heard from you. If he knew where you'd gone."

"I guess I got tired of running away from him." There was a pause, and I knew it cost him something to say it. His voice was still cool. "We had a long talk."

"I'm glad," I said.

"How's your mom?" he asked.

"My mother is joining a convent," I said. "She wants to be a nun."

"No kidding."

"She's already put the house on the market."

"I'll bet that was a shock."

I flushed with relief at the softening of his voice. "I guess. In some weird way it makes perfect sense." Why is this so hard to say? I thought. There was a thickening silence between us that I didn't know how to fill.

"Zoe? My dad just made dinner, and I'd like to eat it while it's hot. If there's nothing else—"

"Wait," I said, clutching the phone.

"Yes?"

"Can't we talk for a minute?"

There was another long silence. "What do you want, Zoe?"

"I thought we could be friends."

"I don't think so."

"Why not?"

"You're too old for me."

I took a deep breath and stood up. "Okay, that hurt." I paced the room, cradling the phone in my arm. "There's no excuse for how I behaved. But my family needed me. I was distracted."

"Bullshit. You looked at me like I was garbage. Like you couldn't wait to get rid of me."

It was true. Everything he said was true. But what made me feel even worse was the way his voice cracked, saying it.

"I'm sorry. I was wrong. I was scared." I wound the phone cord around my finger. "I love you, Paul." To say those words out loud felt like throwing myself off a cliff.

"Excuse me, what did you say?"

"If you want me to leave you alone, I will. But I love you." I felt my heart below my ribs, hurting. It had been a long day. And yet even as I spoke there was a feeling of relief, as if I were laying down a burden, and I felt lighter after the words left my mouth.

"Well." His voice was so quiet I could barely hear it. "I guess that's not what I expected to hear."

My grip tightened on the phone. "When I started this trip I wanted to get away from everything that made me feel bad. I didn't want to be in any more pain. And then I met you and everything happened, the storm, and us, and it felt perfect as long as I could keep it all separate. Distant. Apart from me. I fell in love with you on the river, but I didn't want to admit it."

Paul's voice was ragged. "Why not?"

"I was afraid."

"Of me?"

"Yes. You. You're eleven years younger than I am. You lied to me constantly about nearly everything. Of course I was afraid. I'm terrified of falling in love again with the wrong man."

There was a long sigh from Paul's end. "I always thought love was kind of like swimming."

"Why?"

"You have to get in over your head."

"I didn't want to do that."

"But you did."

I waited for him to say more, but the silence stretched out between us. "Well. I just wanted to let you know," I went on, sounding utterly inane. "Even if we never see each other again." My grip on the phone loosened. I could get over this.

"Where will you go now?" he asked.

"Alaska, maybe." The world was big. It wouldn't be so bad to go on driving around for a while, not knowing what might happen, living with everything that had already happened. "I'll probably fly to Montana, pick up the Winnebago, and head north."

"That's a long drive, Zoe."

Hope flared inside me as the burden of my caution lifted one more time. "You want to come with me?"

"Do you want me to?"

"Yes," I said, smiling into the phone. "I do."

In the Great Falls airport parking lot, the RV was silent and locked, blinds drawn. I found the keys in my purse, unlocked the door, and pulled it open.

A cup and a spoon lay in the sink, rinsed and turned over to dry. The stale smell of coffee hung in the air, sealed in by the insulated walls. The table was empty. The closet door was open, revealing empty space. It seemed as though it had been a hundred years since I'd been here, and it was good to be back.

As I drove toward the river, Montana looked even more lush than I remembered. The wide prairie benches fell off into broad valleys, and the ocean of grass was a darker green than before. The June sun was still high at five o'clock in the afternoon, but the air was chilly, the wind stiff. I let the Winnebago coast off the highway into a turnout next to the Missouri.

I stepped into the back of the cabin, pulled the blinds open and looked out at the river. It felt all right to be alone. The hole that was left by my father's death was more bearable, now. Maybe because it gave me an exit, a tunnel for me to crawl out and find the life I needed. Oddly enough, it was my mother I missed, especially the sight of her solemn, blinking face on the lawn, like an owl who had woken up to find itself in sunlight. In the end she was the one who made it clear to me I was free, free to disappoint people, free to choose a lover or a convent. But it was the freedom that was important.

I opened a window to let in some air. A walk by the river was all I wanted now. Paul was flying up to meet me in Spokane tomorrow, but I still had plenty of time to get there. I could drive all night if I had to. We'd talked about going up through British Columbia to the southern tip of the Yukon, but we didn't have to make any decisions right away. My jeans were folded in the duffel bag, my sneakers tucked under them. I changed quickly, slipped on my jacket and stepped out the door.

Epilogue
Six Months Later

Diamond-shaped panes of sunlight glance off the water and their reflections ripple across the taut belly of sail above me. I am writing. The heat is bright, intense. The only sound is the keening of gulls, the snap of wind on the mainsail and the zipperlike buzz as Paul hoists the spinnaker to take advantage of our tail wind. We're halfway between Aruba and Curaçao, headed for the north coast of Venezuela. We're making good time, although that isn't a priority.

Home for us now is a twenty-eight foot sloop called *Lollipop*—Lolly for short. Paul and I sleep in a bed that curves to fit her hull; we make love to the sound of flying fish slapping the water. We cook in a tiny galley and eat at a table no bigger than the table in the Winnebago; we do well in these tight, moveable rooms.

The Winnebago took us from Juneau to

Miami, where we sold it to a retired couple from Kansas. Paul finally invested the inheritance from his mother in *Lollipop*, although his father never tires of pointing out to us that a boat cannot be considered an investment.

For the past six months I've been scribbling on a story that has consumed about nine legal pads so far. I write in longhand, immersed for hours in memories of our adventures. No matter what becomes of this manuscript, I've loved reliving them. This is my thank you note to life, and the dead who watch over us.

Paul returns to the captain's chair, corrects our course, and props his feet up on the gunwale. "Want to take the helm?" he asks. "I need to check my line."

"Sure," I say, putting down my pen and paper. "Lose your bait again?"

"Probably," he says, and scratches a mosquito bite on his neck.

"Move over," I say, and try to scoot in beside him.

Paul pulls me into his lap and kisses me, then gives me a little shake. "When can I read it?"

"Soon," I laugh. "When it's finished."

"I love you, Zoe," he whispers in my ear. He knows I'm writing about us.

My cheek rests on his head, my arms wrap

around his shoulders. On the far horizon the silhouette of mountains appear, translucent as clouds, at least thirty miles in the distance. I sit up straight.

"Land," I say.

"South America," Paul says.

My pulse quickens; the wind picks up and a thread of salt spray splashes us. The bowsprit lifts and falls and lifts again, lilting, pointing toward the new world.